Bullets in Buzzards Creek

BRET REY

A Black Horse Western

ROBERT HALE • LONDON

Photoset in North Wales by
Derek Doyle & Associates, Mold, Clwyd.
Printed and bound in Great Britain by
WBC Book Manufacturers Limited,
Bridgend, Mid-Glamorgan.

For Marjorie
who first led me down the trail

ONE

Forty-seven year old Doc Rickman started as the hammering on his front door broke the silence. What emergency was in need of his attention at seven o'clock on a Sunday morning, just as he was drying his lean face after shaving?

The frantic knocking continued without cease and he called out, 'I'm coming! There's no need to break the door down!'

He unlocked the door to find Chris Casey, a pimply youth in his early teens, in a state of acute distress. Before the medic could ask what all the fuss was about the boy blurted out, 'Come quick, Doc. There's a woman lyin' in the mud at the back of the Eldorado. She looks all funny.'

'Wait there, Chris. I'll get my coat.'

Black bag in hand, Rickman stepped out smartly alongside the boy, already wondering who the woman could be. Probably some drunken prostitute, he surmised uncharitably.

When they arrived at the rear of the Eldorado Saloon he knew at once that the woman was dead.

7

'Go get the sheriff, son. Quick as you can.'

Chris Casey scampered away and the doc bent over the dead woman and removed the silken shawl knotted tightly around her neck. He felt for a pulse he knew he would not find. The body was already growing cold and stiff.

When Sheriff Jeff Gilpin arrived, with Chris Casey still in tow, Rickman anticipated the question. 'She's been dead four or five hours, Sheriff. Strangled with her own shawl.'

The doc held it out towards him. 'Made of silk. Very strong but very slippery. My guess is that she was knocked unconscious first, then the shawl was used to strangle her. There is heavy bruising on the chin.'

'But you're still only guessin', Doc?'

'That's all I can do, short of any other evidence.'

'Sure, Doc. Thanks.' The sheriff turned to the youth. 'You found the body?'

Chris Casey had never seen a dead body before, but instead of crumbling at the sight of tbe dead woman, he found it exciting.

'Yes, sir. I always take a walk before breakfast on a Sunday. My folks don't get up so early on the Sabbath. I ran and told the doctor as soon as I saw her lying there. I thought she was just sick.'

'Good for you, son. Now will you do me another favour?'

'Sure will.'

'Go an' tell Mr Wragby. He'll know what to do. Then you get back home an' have your breakfast.'

The rain had ceased but the dead woman's clothing was heavily soaked. Sheriff Gilpin had no reason to doubt the doctor's assessment about the time of death. Between two and four in the dead of night, when all self-respecting folks were asleep.

'Who is she, Doc?'

'I think she's one of Moe Langley's girls.'

'Thought I was right. The last one to arrive in town. Jennie, I think her name is.'

'Then why did you ask me?'

Gilpin smiled through his abundant, well-trimmed beard. 'Just wanted confirmation, but we'd best get her formally identified. Could you spare the time to go an' see Moe an' break the news to her? I'd best stay with the body 'til Josh gets here.'

'I'll do that, Sheriff, then I'll get home to my breakfast. If you want me to examine the body more fully later, just give me a call.'

'Will do. After church suit you?'

'That will do nicely.'

Gilpin was acutely aware that Buzzards Creek was a town to which death was no stranger. Gunfights and the victims of arson had all come his way during the past three years, and this was the second woman to be strangled in the town within a few weeks. Men getting killed was nothing new in Western townships, but death was breaking new ground in Buzzards Creek with the murder of women.

Had this girl been killed on the spot or carried here from the scene of her murder and left? The bulging eyes and the discoloured features made it difficult to tell how old she had been.

There were no age lines around the eyes and mouth, suggesting early twenties, which was about the age she had seemed to Gilpin on the rare occasions he had seen her in the Eldorado. Saloon girls came to town and went away again fairly regularly. He had paid little attention to her in life, but in death she would become far more significant. As if he hadn't enough on his plate already with the feud going on between the factions staking claim to the ranch and town property of the deceased Roger Talbot.

If this young woman had been killed on the spot, what had she been doing abroad at such an early hour?

It seemed likely that she had not been to bed, or at least not the one reserved for her at the Eldorado, so where had she spent the last hour of Saturday and the beginning of Sunday?

And who would want to kill a saloon girl, other than some man she had spurned? Finding out who she might have offended could eat away a lot of the sheriff's hours.

He looked around in the muddy alley for footprints, recalling that rain had begun to fall just before midnight. Old tracks would probably have been washed away when the storm was at its fiercest, but there was clear evidence of where Chris Casey had stepped, his smaller feet going in several directions, leading back and forth to the doctor's house and then the jail. The doctor's prints were also clearly defined and so were the sheriff's own. But there were no footprints of the victim.

'Mornin', Josh,' the sheriff greeted the carpenter-undertaker as he arrived with his buckboard, young Casey with him, in spite of Gilpin's instruction to go home for his breakfast. The sheriff understood the boy's curiosity and said nothing.

Wragby got down from his buckboard. 'What have we gotten, Jeff?' He looked down at the body. 'Poor Jennie,' he said sadly.

'You knew her?'

'Yeah. One of Moe's girls. Not been here more than a couple of months. Took one chance too many, I guess.'

Afraid the conversation would be inhibited with the boy listening, Gilpin told him, 'You'd best get off home now Chris. Me an' Mr Wragby can manage now.'

The boy stared back, reluctant to leave, but then muttered, 'All right, Sheriff.'

'An' don't go gossipin' about this, not to anyone. You wouldn't want to hinder my investigation now, would you?'

'No, sir. I won't say a word.'

The sheriff didn't believe him. Young Chris would blurt out every detail to his parents as they sat around the breakfast table.

As soon as the boy was out of earshot the sheriff's gaze again settled on Josh Wragby. 'What d'you mean, one chance too many?'

'She liked men and men liked her, only Moe don't encourage her girls to fraternize outside the Four

Aces. Jennie resented the restriction. I know she's slipped out more than a few times to meet a man.'

'How d'you know that?'

'Because she came to my house a couple of times after midnight.'

'Recently?'

· Wragby's steady gaze wavered, then shifted to the dead girl again. 'No. Not for three weeks or more.' He paused reflectively. 'I guess she needed a younger man. She was only twenty.'

The friendship between a girl of twenty and a man Gilpin knew was well past forty gave him food for thought, but it wasn't hard to guess what the older man was hinting at. It was the simple fact of a girl less than half his age striking up such a personal relationship with the carpenter that surprised him.

'You never married, did you, Josh?'

'No. Never felt the need. Always got by with the occasional bit of fun. When you've put as many folks to rest as I have the human body seems less important than it does to most folks, I guess. But I'm right sorry about this one. She was so full of the joy of living. Right pretty, she was.'

There was a small silence, until Wragby said, 'Let's get her back to my place.'

TWO

Maybe the Casey boy had talked, in spite of his promise to keep quiet, or it could have been the girls from Moe Langley's saloon, but somehow the news of Jennie Clark's murder had spread rapidly around the town. The Rev'd John Brunton had informed the sheriff that he would have something to say about it in his sermon that morning, although he had declined to reveal from where he had gotten his information.

'Confidentiality is something which is too often broken these days, Sheriff.'

The preacher had strode off to the church to make his preparations and, less than an hour later, the street was full of people heading for the church. Normally the building with its little steeple was half empty, but when Gilpin decided to join the congregation, more out of curiosity about what Brunton would have to say than for any religious feelings, he found only two seats unoccupied. He looked around, then took one of then.

Brunton delivered a hard-hitting sermon to the kind of numbers he had always wanted to see sitting there for the last hour of a Sunday morning. After the opening hymn, prayers and a Bible reading, followed by another hymn, he wasted neither words nor time.

'This very morning another young woman was found murdered in our town, further evidence of the evil within our midst. I challenge every single one of you to search your conscience, to ask yourselves why we cannot live here in peace and safety, surrounded by such beautiful country.

'This town of ours could be a Garden of Eden if every man, woman and child would only obey those Ten Commandments handed down to us through the centuries. We should be thanking the good Lord for giving us a wonderful guide for living.'

As the pastor paused for effect, the silence was complete. Every ear awaited his next words, though not every eye found the courage to meet his searching gaze. There was no doubting his power to bewitch his listeners. Sheriff Gilpin wondered how many consciences would be pricked.

'When heartless men take a pride in killing each other we can put it down to perverted male ego, but when the victims of murder are young women I tremble with shame for the future of mankind.'

Another short pause for emphasis, not too long, but just long enough to make everyone wait with bated breath for what was yet to come. Sure evidence of the true orator.

Gilpin noticed Brunton's eyes resting on Moe Langley as he continued. 'Is there no way to control this wickedness going on around us? Must we continue to allow women of loose morals to corrupt our young men, to tempt husbands to betray their wives, to spread discontent and the ultimate decay of family life?'

Someone coughed and the little church almost shook.

'What fiendish evil drives a citizen of Buzzards Creek to strangle a young woman? What are we going to do to try and discover who is responsible for such crimes? This is the second of the fair sex to depart this world within a few weeks in similar circumstances. Not one of you has offered Sheriff Gilpin the slightest help in finding Molly Shaw's killer.'

His eyes roamed over every person there, hard and challenging.

'Will one of you ladies sitting here this morning be the next victim?

'I urge you all to question the whereabouts of your menfolk during the early hours of this Sabbath. If you have reason to suspect anyone, I plead with you to pass on any information which may be of help to Sheriff Gilpin. Until this mystery is solved – and it seems likely that this latest killing was perpetrated by the same man who strangled Molly Shaw – we must all live with the nightmare possibility of another life being lost in the same way.'

The pastor then invited them all to bow their heads while he prayed 'for the soul of our poor departed sister'.

At the end of the service everyone sat in silence while the Rev'd John Brunton made his way to the door, to stand outside and shake the hand of each worshipper as they left for home.

The sheriff stood and watched them go. Moe Langley and all her girls, Josh Wragby, young Chris Casey and his parents, Chet Handley, the lumber merchant, Frank Walmsley, blacksmith, Bob Reid, saddler, and his wife. Valerie Underwood, who owned the Rooming House, was there, along with Doc Rickman. Not a single candidate for murder among them, Gilpin mused.

When only the preacher and the sheriff remained the former asked, 'Which one of them do you suspect, Sheriff?'

'None of them, Mr Brunton, but I guess until the killer is found I'll have to suspect every one of 'em. You see what I'm up against?'

'I do indeed, and I wish you well with your investigation.'

'Right now only God an' the killer himself knows who did it.'

'I don't think either one is going to tell you, Sheriff.'

'Pity you ain't gotten a direct line to the Almighty, John.'

'Unfortunately I'm not Moses.'

That you're not, Gilpin silently said to himself as he walked back to his office.

'Come in!' Moe Langley called in answer to the

knock on her office door. 'Hello, there, Sheriff,' she greeted as Gilpin entered and closed the door behind him.

She glanced at the gun hanging low at his right hip. 'I see this is an official visit. I thought you looked almost naked in church this morning without your gun.'

'I was kind o' surprised t'see you there with all your girls.'

'You think because I keep a saloon I'm a heathen?' she challenged.

Something approaching a smile appeared between the moustache and the lush growth of beard. 'You ain't tryin' t'tell me you go regularly?'

She hesitated before replying. 'No, I don't. But after the doc told me about Jennie, I felt the need. I took the girls along as a mark of respect to a dead colleague. You might not believe it, Sheriff, but I was brought up in a very religious way.'

He wondered how she had strayed so far from such an upbringing, but it was not the time to ask.

'What can you tell me about Jennie?'

'Jennie Clark. Came to me three or four months ago.' Longer than Josh Wragby had estimated, Gilpin noted, but he did not interrupt her. 'There'd been some trouble in Sacramento with two men. I gather they both decided to claim territorial rights. One of them killed the other. After they had a hanging party Jennie wasn't very popular. Woman who employed her decided Buzzards Creek was far enough away to give the girl a fresh start and asked me to give her a chance.'

'But Jennie couldn't change,' Gilpin mused aloud.

'What do you mean?'

'She liked men. Mebbe she needed a man. An' you laid down rules she couldn't or wouldn't obey.'

Moe Langley's eyes lowered and she fiddled with a pencil, steeling herself to make the admission that gave her no credit and brought her only a sense of humiliation.

'I didn't know that. Not until this morning.'

'Somebody must've known.'

'Oh yes, some people knew.' Her voice hardened. 'What kind of a fool do you think that makes me look? I'm supposed to be smart, but she was smarter. She went to bed every night like a good girl, then when everybody else was asleep she'd creep out of the back door and meet some man. Come back before sun-up, making sure she locked the door again before she sneaked back up to bed. This morning when Hilda came down . . .'

'Your cook-housekeeper,' Gilpin interjected.

'. . . the back door wasn't locked. That's when I went to check on the girls, making sure they were all there.'

'And they were all there except Jennie?'

'Right. No wonder that girl always slept late.'

'But you didn't know she was dead then?'

'No. Doc Rickman came in a few minutes afterwards and told me. I just didn't want to believe it. It was a terrible shock.'

She looked into his sombre eyes. 'I've seen men

die in gunfights, women beaten up, but this . . . strangled with her own shawl. . . .'

Her voice trailed away, the shock of Jennie's
murder still overwhelming her. Tough and worldly-
wise she might be, hard-headed enough to come to
Buzzards Creek and build a new saloon and bordello
on the sight where Roger Talbot had been shot and
then charred in the conflagration of his cherished
Gold Dust House, but Jeff Gilpin knew he was seeing
her soul bared as few others ever would.

He remained silent, patiently waiting until she
regained control of her emotions.

'She's the second woman to be strangled in
Buzzards Creek in the last few weeks,' she reminded
herself. 'Like the preacher said, which one of us will
be next?'

The sheriff shrugged. 'Do any of the girls know
who Jennie was meeting last night?'

'Rita thinks it was Bob Reid, but she's not sure.
Cecille thinks she'd been offered another job, either
down at the Eldorado or with Sean Murphy at the
Stags Head.'

'I know Sean. He wouldn't entice her out for a job
interview at that hour. Besides, you know as well as I
do that Sean is dead against any of his girls gettin'
too close to the customers.'

'I have heard that.'

'An' Bob Reid is a married man. He certainly
wouldn't have entertained Jennie in his own home.'

'His wife would have known if he'd been out of the
house.'

'Exactly. Would you mind if I talk to your girls?'

'You'll talk to them whether I like it or not, but thanks for asking. Maybe they'll tell you more than they've told me.'

He had already decided that was a strong possibility, but it turned out they knew very little about Jennie Clark's men friends. They could do a lot of guessing, but hard facts were simply not available. All they had to go on were the intimate glances between Jennie and a number of patrons of the Four Aces, but it was her job to be pleasant to the customers, so just how much intimate glances meant was anybody's guess. But at least it would be worthwhile talking to a few men whose names had cropped up.

The only inkling of a clue had come from Cecille. When the sheriff had asked her why she thought Jennie had been offered another job she told him the dead girl had said, 'Don't you worry about me, Cecille. I'll be out of here a week from now.'

A new job in the offing or what? Had some infatuated rancher asked for her hand in marriage, besotted to the point where he didn't give a damn about the men she might have bedded before?

Gilpin didn't think it likely, but he could hardly afford to dismiss anything at that stage.

THREE

He was on his way back to his office when a rider dismounted and tied his mount to the rail, then looked around him. Gilpin could scarcely believe his eyes as he recognized the tall, skinny man with the thick, wide blond moustache and sparkling pale blue eyes that fastened on him. The city clothes, pants pushed into riding boots, the narrow bow tie and the bulge under his coat on the right hip were almost like a uniform. The two men smiled at each other as they drew close and held out their hands in greeting.

'John Henry Holliday! What in hell brings you to Buzzards Creek?'

'On my way south, Jeff. Thought I'd look you up.'

'Glad you did. Come on in. I'll rustle up some coffee.'

As Gilpin stepped up on to the stoop Holliday said. 'I could use something a mite stronger, if you have it?'

Gilpin turned. 'The saloon?'

'I sure have me a thirst, Sheriff. That trail was mighty dusty.'

21

'We'll go to the Stags Head. Owner is a friend o' mine. Good Irishman. You'll like Sean.'

Sean Murphy was nowhere around so they ambled to the bar and Holliday ordered a bottle and two glasses, took them to a vacant table and poured two generous shots of whiskey.

'Go easy there, Doc! I have to limit my drinkin' these days.'

'How come? You sick or something?'

'I'm county sheriff. Have to set an example. Wouldn't do for me to stumble around town in a drunken stupor.'

Holliday was suddenly smitten with a bout of hard coughing. When it was over he took a swig of the fiery liquor and croaked, 'You mean you can't hold your liquor no more.'

'If you want to put it that way. Now tell me, where are you headed an' what you been doin' since we were in Dodge together?'

'Hell, Jeff, that seems like half a lifetime ago. I wouldn't know where to start.'

Gilpin was tempted to ask about 'Big Nose' Kate, who was Holliday's concubine in the old days, but prudence got the better of his curiosity.

'Seems to me you're a bit off the beaten track, John. If you're headed south I'd have thought you'd take the train.'

Holliday shrugged away the inference and said, 'Matter of fact, I heard you'd been shot a while back. Decided to come and find out first hand.'

'It was nothin'. Bullet from a Derringer, fired close

up. I was back in harness in no time. Feller by the name o' Joe Blondell agreed to be deputised. . . .'

'Joe Blondell? Gambling man?'

'That's the one, You know him?'

'I've taken money off of him a time or two, but he's a smart gambler, that Joe. Never figured on him toting a star.'

'He was a mite reluctant an' that's fact. It wasn't for long.'

The Doc poured himself more whiskey and drank appreciatively.

'You're lookin' good, John,' Gilpin lied through his teeth. 'How've you bin?'

'Reckon this is one of my good days. I've made those doctors who gave me two years to live back in seventy-three look stupid.'

But for how much longer, Gilpin mused, seeing the sickly pallor of Holliday's face. 'I guess so,' he said.

'You keep a quiet town these days, Jeff?'

The sheriff shook his head. 'Do my best, but seems there's allus some varmint ready to make trouble. Had two women strangled right here in town in the past few weeks an' I still ain't gotten a clue as to who the killer is. On top o' that there's feuds goin' on about who should inherit the property left by a dead man who refused to make a Will. Figured he had plenty o' time an' had nobody particular in mind to inherit.'

'Roger Talbot?'

'You have been well informed. Yeah, he owned the

biggest ranch in the county, several properties in town, includin' the Gold Dust House that got burnt to the ground, with him inside it.'

'Couldn't be a problem about that then.'

'Nope. We'd no sooner gotten the site cleaned up than along comes a woman bv the name o' Moe Langley with enough ready money to build a new whorehouse on the same site.'

Looking around the room Holliday said, 'This place don't look much like a whorehouse.'

'It ain't. No roulette wheel, no faro. Sean allows poker, but this is a place where decent folks can come for a quiet drink and a smile from girls who are employed just to add a little brightness t'the place. If you want a game, John, you'll have to visit the Eldorado or The Four Aces.'

Holliday lifted the bottle again and held it poised as he looked at Gilpin's glass. 'You're not drinking, Jeff.'

'Enough in there for me, but you go ahead, John, if you've a mind. Reckon you'll sleep well after you've finished that bottle.'

'This place is too quiet for sleep.'

Gilpin knew what Holliday meant. The gambler with a reputation with both knife and gun was accustomed to a more noisy atmosphere.

'It's Sunday, Doc. The stores are closed all day. Folks keep the Sabbath as a day o' rest hereabouts.'

'Apart from the saloons, huh?'

'An' the Eating House. Travellers need to fill their bellies an' slake their thirst, even on the Sabbath.'

As if to contradict what Gilpin had quietly stated, a sudden outbreak of gunfire shattered the silence and the sheriff leapt to his feet, heading for the door.

Outside he saw gunsmoke wafting away on the still air and guns being reholstered as a group of men dismounted and hitched their horses to the rail outside The Four Aces. Gilpin recognized none of them. Troublemakers, he sighed, and knew he had to do something about it.

He ambled down the street, John Henry Holliday forgotten, but his old friend sensed he might need some help and the man known as 'Doc' was quietly trailing him.

The sheriff stood just inside the doorway and looked over the seven men lined up against the bar, unaware of his entrance. Eventually one of them turned and noticed the star on Gilpin's vest. He put on a big smile and said, 'Well whadaya know boys, this town's gotten itself a sheriff.'

The others swung around and laughter gurgled in their throats. One of them said, 'Reckon he don't know about you an' lawmen, Rube.'

'Reckon not,' Rube said. 'You wanna tell him, Grover?'

'Sure, why not?' The one called Grover switched his gaze back to Gilpin. 'Rube, here, kills lawmen for the fun of it. He don't mind if they're town marshals or county sheriffs, they all come the same to Rube.'

'That why you came t'town, mister?' Gilpin asked Rube.

'Not exactly, Sheriff. We're jest passin' through. Rustled ourselves up a thirst on the trail, is all.'

'Then what's with all that gunplay out there?'

'Town seemed kinda dead, so we figured we'd liven it up a bit. Didn't know you were here, mind, but now you are, what you aim to do about it?'

'We like our town quiet on a Sunday, so when you've slaked your thirst, get back on those horses an' keep ridin'.'

As if by long accustomed practice they all turned their backs on him, lifted their glasses and appeared to ignore him. He took two steps closer. 'Shouldn't take you more'n ten minutes,' he told them.

The man Rube turned around slowly. 'We'll take as long as we like, Mister Sheriff, an' if you don't like it, what are ya gonna do about it?'

At the sound of what the others knew was the prelude to gunplay, they all spread out in a new moon formation and stood watching the exchanges. Gilpin knew he was now facing seven potential killers instead of one, but he had never backed down in his life.

He said, 'I'll lock you up for disturbin' the peace.'

Rube took two paces forward. 'Over my dead body.'

'If necessary, yes.'

It was just the challenge Rube wanted and Gilpin knew it. The thrill of battle he had never been able to understand, pitting his skill with a gun against a man too sure of himself, surged through him, the almost righteous sense that he was about to avenge the killings this man had notched up urging him on. The excitement of another gunfight in the cause of justice. He had enough confidence in his ability to win it and chance whether the bravado of the others would crumble when they saw their leader lying dead on the floor.

Rube's hands flashed to the twin-holstered guns on his hips, intent on adding another scalp to his list of dead lawmen, only he hadn't reckoned on Gilpin's response. By the time the snouts of Rube's guns had cleared leather his body was hurled backwards. Two bullets fron Gilpin's Peacemaker Colt had thudded into him, all Rube's control nullified by shock, his eyes declaring amazement as both guns clattered to the board floor, then slowly the sight dimmed and his eyelids shuttered as he slumped forward in death, face down.

The other six stared in stupefaction at the body of their leader, unable to comprehend that such a fate could have befallen him. Then in unison their right hands moved, eager to avenge the death of Rube, in spite of having Gilpin's gun aimed at them. Away to their left, in the uncanny silence that had settled on the gunsmoke, a quiet voice spoke one word of command. 'Don't!'

Their heads swivelled sideways to see a tall man with blond hair holding a Colt .45 aimed in their direction.

'Butt out, mister!' one of them said. 'This ain't none o' your business.'

'Wrong. The sheriff is a friend of mine.'

'And who the hell are you?'

'They call me Doc Holliday.'

Their mouths fell open. Two severe shocks in as many minutes was too much for them all.

'Doc Holliday!' Grover whispered, his throat suddenly gone dry.

'Let's get outa here!' another of the gang said earnestly. 'I ain't tanglin' with Doc Holliday.'

Sheriff Gilpin said, 'That's good advice, fellers. Either that or there'll be six more dead men clutterin' up this place.'

Their eyes wandered from one to the other as if they were trying to make up their minds to swallow their pride and live, or take the chance that maybe one or two of them might survive in a gun battle with these two men. None of them wanted to risk it, even with odds of six to two in their favour. There was no telling which of them would get lucky.

One of them stepped forward, hands now low at his sides. 'Jest so you'll know me next time, Sheriff, I'm Grover Nichols, an' I'll be back when you ain't gotten this gunslinger to back you up.'

'Thanks for the warnin'. I'll be waitin'.'

Grover Nichols led the way outside, the sheriff and his friend not far behind them. The two men watched the six mount their horses and ride south, fast.

'Thanks, John. I didn't figure on them takin' a chance after I'd killed the one they'd called Rube. I had him pegged as their leader an' with him dead I'd banked on 'em all crumblin'.' He glanced sideways at

Holliday. 'You must've come in through the back way.'

'I did, and you were right. Rube Pullen was their leader. I've seen him before. Outlaw gang. Had it not been Sunday I'd have said they rode in to rob the bank, but as it is, I guess maybe they were just passing through.'

'If they come back, they might have a go at the bank. I'd best be prepared.'

He turned his gaze from the departing riders back to Holliday as men began to appear on the street to find out what all the noise was about. 'I might've gotten one or two of 'em, but without you to back me I reckon I could've been dead now.'

'Goes with the job, Sheriff. If you want to die of old age you'd best turn in your badge.'

FOUR

The trouble with killings of the kind meted out to Molly Shaw and Jennie Clark was the lack of any real evidence. Apart from the manner in which they had died and the fact that both bodies had been found at the back of the Eldorado, short of getting a confession, how can you get proof against anybody you might suspect? Assuming the killer was the same man in both cases, then it could be that the residents of Buzzards Creek had a maniac in their midst, only Sheriff Gilpin knew of no madman in the town or on the surrounding ranches. He would have to ask the same questions he had already put in his efforts to track down Molly Shaw's killer, only this time he had been given a few hints as to who might be suspect.

He decided it would be better to interview Bob Reid in his workshop, which would mean postponing it until the morning, but Gilpin had no such reservations concerning Rex Neeson, the tall, strongly-built, ginger-haired owner of the Eldorado Saloon. A girl like Jennie Clark would have been putty in his hands.

Leading the way up to his office with unconcealed

reluctance, Neeson seated himself behind his desk as Gilpin took a chair without waiting for an invitation.

'What's so important that you want to discuss it in private, Sheriff?'

'What time did Jennie Clark leave here this mornin'?'

'What makes you think she was here? She works for Moe Langley, as you should well know.'

'I heard on good authority that you were tryin' to woo her away from The Four Aces. She had an appointnent t'see you after midnight, when everybody else would be a-bed.'

'Is that what they're saying?'

'That's what they're sayin'. That much I can prove. You want t'deny it?'

Neeson stared back at the sheriff with obvious annoyance. It was clear that he was surprised by Gilpin's knowledge of the assignation, but if the sheriff had proof there was no point in contradicting him.

'She came to me for a job. She was sick of working for Moe, with all the restrictions she puts on her girls.'

'The only restriction Moe Langley puts on her girls is that they earn their money in The Four Aces an' not outside.'

His eyes locked on the sheriff in plain antagonism, Neeson asked, 'So what d'you want from me?'

'I want to know what time she got here, what happened between you, an' what time she left.'

Rex Neeson leaned back in his chair, hands held at

the back of his head, and assumed an attitude of supreme confidence.

'It was close to one o'clock when she arrived. All my girls were in bed. We talked about what would be expected of her if she came to work for me and what would be in it for her. She was here no more than twenty minutes.'

'Where did she go from here?'

'How the hell would I know?' Neeson snarled back, letting the front legs of his chair thump forward on the floor. 'I thought she'd go back to The Four Aces, but from what happened to her it's obvious she was meeting some man.'

'Who let her out o' here? You?'

'Of course. I told you, my girls were all in bed.'

'Didn't you watch which way she went?'

'No, I didn't. It was raining out there.'

'So you're tellin' me you let her out, locked up an' went t'bed?'

'Right.'

'But you can't prove it.'

'Do I have to?'

'Rumour has it you'd gotten the hots for her. Was that why you wanted her here? I'd have thought you'd gotten enough girls without adding another to the brothel. Or were you plannin' to get rid o' one of 'em?'

A sardonic smile betrayed contempt for the sheriff's suggestion. 'You're clutching at straws. Sheriff, same as you were when Molly Shaw was killed.'

'How about this for a scenario then. You told her

what you expected from her, hinting she should show you if she was all you thought she might be, then when she played hard t'get you lost your temper, which we all know has a short fuse. Then you strangled her an' dumped the body out in the back alley?'

'If I'd wanted Jennie Clark for my own personal pleasure, what reason would I have to kill her?'

'I've just told you. She didn't cotton to the idea.'

Neeson was affronted by the suggestion than any woman would turn him down, but he could see that to anyone else it would seem like a most unusual hour for a girl to be interviewed for a job. He leaned forward, put on a smile and an air of confidentiality.

'We're both men of the world, Sheriff. You've been around. Jennie was a real good looker. Young. Sure I fancied her and I'd heard she was obliging, if you know what I mean?'

Gilpin did. 'So you hit the sack together, is that what you're sayin'?'

'Sure we did. She could've stayed all night if she'd wanted, only she said she needed to think things over.'

The sheriff remained silent, waiting for Neeson to go on.

Neeson shrugged. 'So she was here for more than twenty minutes. More like an hour, I guess, but would I kill her after that?'

Gilpin said nothing in reply. The time element was rapidly dwindling. If what Neeson said was true, that the girl had not arrived until one o'clock and stayed for an hour, her death had occurred shortly after-wards, assuming that Doc Rickman was right in his assessment of the time of death. Had someone been waiting for Jennie as she energed from the Eldorado? Someone who had known she would be there?

It was still early in the evening when Gilpin emerged from the Eldorado and saw Walt Martin riding into town. The rancher spotted him thirty seconds later and, instead of dismounting outside the Sheriff's Office as he had intended, he rode forward to halt alongside the sheriff. Gilpin sensed his arrival spelled more trouble.

'What brings you into town of a Sunday evenin', Walt?'

'I've gotten visitors, Sheriff.'

'That look on your face tells me they ain't exactly welcome. Am I right?'

'I'm not sure . . . yet.'

'Who are these visitors?'

'Can we talk in your office?'

'Sure, come along.'

While the sheriff unlocked the door the prema-turely grey Walt Martin hitched his roan gelding to the rail. Long legs followed the sheriff into his office and stretched out from the chair Gilpin invited his visitor to take. Martin's usually cheerful, friendly countenance was wearing a grave expression.

Gilpin wondered what Martin wanted with him. 'So tell me about your visitors, Walt.'

'Woman in her thirties with a son thirteen years

old. She says Roger Talbot was his father and she's laying claim to the ranch on behalf of the boy.'

'She gotten any proof about this?'

'A birth certificate. It says mother Laura Parker, father Roger Talbot.'

'An' you think it's a forgery?'

'It might be, I've no way of knowing.'

'Seems like you need Eli Atkins to sort out this one, Walt, so why come t'me?'

'They've gotten a man with them. Calls himself Horace Idle. He's a gunny, I'd stake my life on it.'

That put a whole new complexion on what had at first seemed like a normal claim to inherit a dead man's property.

'This, er, Idle . . . he made any threats?'

'None. I reckon he could charm the birds off the trees, but there's something underneath it all, I'm certain of it. This woman has brought him to make sure she gets what she wants.'

Gilpin knew that Walt Martin was not a fanciful man, but. . . .

'That's speculation, Walt, don't you reckon?'

Martin shrugged. 'It's a gut feeling, Sheriff. I can't prove it, but as far as I'm concerned that man is a threat. I'm no gunman, as you well know. Neither do I employ gunmen, so I guess I may need your help. That's why I rode in, to give you fair warning. I know Eli will have to sort out the legal implications and I might find myself out of a job, but I don't intend to just lie down and accept this woman's claim if she's a fraud.'

'What have you told 'em?'

'I've invited them to stay the night and told them we'll have to sort it out with Talbot's lawyer in the morning.'

'How did they react to that?'

'Agreed without a qualm. "Best if it's all settled nice and legal" the woman said.'

The sheriff could understand Martin's fears to some extent. Since Roger Talbot had died intestate, Walt had continued to manage the ranch as he had during Talbot's lifetime and was laying claim to it unless and until some relative showed up with entitlement. He had put several years hard work into making the ranch prosperous, which was what Talbot had hired him to do in the first place. Talbot had known nothing about ranching: he was only interested in money and property.

He had been a shrewd judge of men and had seen the wisdom of hiring Walt Martin, a man of impeccable honesty.

'Don't see there's much I can do unless this Idle feller makes trouble for you, Walt.'

'I know. I just wanted you to be fully aware of what's going on. Maybe you could look him over when they come into town?'

'I'd've done that anyway. Walt.'

Martin climbed to his feet. 'Well, I'd best be getting back. Don't want to leave them in the house on their own for too long. Expect they've been wondering why I had to come into town before supper on a Sunday. No sense in letting them get the idea I'm suspicious.'

'I'll look out for you in the mornin' then. Expect you'll be comin' in with 'em?'

'I will. Thanks for your time, Sheriff.'

'Any time, Walt.'

At least something was happening, Gilpin mused, sitting at his desk in contemplation after Martin had left. If only Roger Talbot had made a Will, as Eli Atkins had advised him, the undercurrent of unrest in and around Buzzards Creek would never have started simmering. Gilpin had long held the opinion that somebody would die before the mess Talbot had left behind him was resolved.

FIVE

The news that 'Doc' Holliday had hit town spread like a high summer forest fire and Moe Langley lost no time inviting John Henry to deal faro in The Four Aces that night. Even men who normally stayed home of a Sunday evening made a beeline for the saloon, just to get a glimpse of this famous dentist who had set aside his implements in favour of making his living as a high stakes gambler. They were surprised to find he was a quiet, modest man with a smile that was almost child-like, in sharp contrast to their preconceived notion of what his reputation as a killer had fixed in their minds. He gave the impression he wouldn't hurt a fly, but legend had spread of his deadly accuracy with both knife and gun and the hard cases he had killed. 'Doc' Holliday proved to be something of a disappointment to most of them, but Moe Langley was not complaining. Bar takings were more than double that of her usual Sunday evening.

The evening passed almost as quietly as any other, with most of the punters going away losing, though not heavily enough to provoke any serious resentment. John Henry Holliday was the last man left in the bar room, apart from the apron, and Moe Langley offered him a room for the night.

'That's right civil of you, ma'am, but I've gotten me a room at the Regal Hotel.'

'It's after midnight, Doc. Hotel will be all closed up.'

'Then I reckon I'll have to hammer on the door until they let me in.'

'You'd be a lot more comfortable with one of my girls.'

The easy smile stretched the wide moustache even further. 'I reckon I might at that, only I'm choosey as to who I share a bed with.'

'Take your pick. If you've gotten any worries I've a new girl who came in only two days ago. Nice and clean, if you know what I mean.'

'Thank you, ma'am, I appreciate the invite, but it's been a long day. Maybe some other night. All I want right now is to fall asleep and not wake until noon. I'll bid you goodnight, ma'am.'

'Goodnight, Doc. See you tomorrow?'

'You might at that.'

Sheriff Jeff Gilpin was tucked up in bed, sleeping the sleep of the righteous, long before John Henry Holliday finished his one o'clock in the morning bout of coughing, but he was up and stretching hours before his old friend. He washed and dressed, ran a comb through his neatly trimmed beard and moustache, then eased the tangles out of his mousy hair, parted in the middle and yet still falling forward to almost completely cover his forehead.

As he ate his breakfast over at the Eating House he contemplated the day ahead. There were men to interview in connection with the killing of Jennie Clark and it was simply a question of deciding in which order he should visit them. He must also remember he had promised Walt Martin he would run his eye over Horace Idle when he rode into town with the woman and child he had escorted to the ranch. There could be trouble ahead for Walt Martin which would probably mean Gilpin himself getting involved.

He decided his first call should be at the livery stables. George Taggart was one of the most affable and popular men in Buzzards Creek and a mine of information. He would know which men had been closely associated with the murdered Jennie Clark.

'Want your horse, Sheriff?'

'Not right now, George. Just a little chat.'

'About what?'

'Jennie Clark. I believe you got to know her better than most.'

'I dunno about that. There was nothing going on between me and Jennie, if that's what you're suggesting?'

'No, I'm not. But I do know you're popular with women.'

Taggart was unsure what the sheriff was intimating. 'You surely don't rate me a suspect?'

'No, George, I don't, but you might know who she

took a shine to. I'm told she liked men, an' not just for the money she could make out of 'em.'

Taggart relaxed. 'The rumours were flying around thick and fast last night, just like they were when Molly Shaw was strangled. Folks reckon the same man killed them both, Sheriff, but to my mind there's no guarantee the two murders are connected.'

In Gilpin's mind the fact that the same method had been used in both killings pointed to the same killer, but he was keeping an open mind.

'Who d'you think killed Molly, George?'

'My money is on Neeson. The girls think she'd gotten something on him and. . . .'

Gilpin's eyes registered mild surprise as he cut in. 'You mean she was puttin' the bite on him?'

'That's my feeling, though what it could be I've no idea.'

Neeson would not have the same motive to do away with Jennie Clark and Gilpin could see why Taggart doubted the two women had been murdered by the same man; whoever had killed Jennie had maybe wanted to give that impression, which might account for Jennie's body being left in the same spot, although it did not necessarily follow that she had been strangled there.

'Tell me, George, who did Jennie take a shine to?'

'That's a leading question, Sheriff. I wouldn't want to finger anybody when there's no real evidence.'

'I know how you feel, an' I won't let what you tell me influence my thinkin' too much, but I need somewhere to start.'

Taggart was reluctant to mention names and Gilpin waited patiently while the livery man battled with his conscience, his civic duty in conflict with his fear of being instrumental in getting the wrong man accused.

'That Jennie was a bit of a tease, Sheriff.'

'But who in particular did she tease?'

'Josh Wragby, Bob Reid, Harry Digweed, and a few others.'

Gilpin did not reveal that he already knew about the relationship between the girl and Josh Wragby, but Moe Langley had also mentioned Bob Reid. He'd better tackle the saddler next.

'Thanks, George. See you later.'

Bob Reid was a little man, reserved, and not the kind to appeal all that much to women. He had a wife and four children and he worked long hours to keep his family provided with the bare necessities, repairing tack as well as making new.

That did not, in Gilpin's mind, indicate he could not be smitten by a younger woman. One night a week, always a Saturday, Reid relaxed in The Four Aces saloon, quietly, without getting inebriated. One of Moe's girls had mentioned that he seemed to have the hots for Jennie Clark and the girl knew it. She had teased him to the point where other customers had noticed and joshed him about it.

'Play your cards right, Bob, an' she'll help you celebrate your birthday,' two of the girls had overheard one man say.

Reid was busy with needle and thread when the sheriff called. Gilpin wasted no time in getting straight to the point.

'Where were you at two o'clock Sunday mornin', Mr Reid?'

The saddler looked him straight in the eye, needle held steadily in mid-air, wondering what lay behind the question.

'Where any self-respecting man would be . . . in bed.'

'Would your wife be willin' to confirm that?'

'Why should she?' Reid demanded indignantly.

'Because I'd like to ask her.'

'Now look here, Sheriff, don't you go getting the idea you can go around prying into people's private lives just because you've gotten that star pinned to your vest, because you can't. I told you I was in bed at two o'clock yesterday morning and you'll have to take my word for it.'

'But you can't prove it,' Gilpin countered quietly.

Reid's voice rose in heightened anger, his eyes glaring. 'I don't have to!'

'You do unless you want me to suspect you of killin' Jennie Clark.'

The saddler tossed down his needle and thread and stood up threateningly. He pointed his right forefinger at Gilpin. 'You go right ahead and suspect as much as you like, you can't prove a thing, except that *somebody* killed her. And another thing, what motive would I have for strangling a saloon girl? Now get the hell out of here!'

Motive for the killing was probably the one aspect that could lead Gilpin to the killer, he surmised.

'Thanks for your time, Mr Reid,' he responded calmly. 'Pity you're not willin' to help catch a killer – and the worst kind o' killer at that.'

As he walked out of the saddlery he couldn't decide if the man was genuinely offended by the request to give himself an alibi or if Reid really did have something to hide. Even if Reid had agreed to let him talk to his wife the odds were that she would probably have confirmed his presence, true or not, and the likelihood was that Reid *had* been in the marital bed at the relevant time.

Lumber worker Harry Digweed had no such reservations. His wife had been dead for more than two years, a victim of consumption, so there was no one he could call on to confirm that he, too, had been in bed at the estimated time of Jennie Clark's death.

'Did Jennie Clark ever visit you at home, Harry?'

A tantalizing smile creased Digweed's face. 'Now that would've given folks something to talk about, wouldn't it?'

The sheriff shrugged. 'Who would see her if she came after midnight?'

'Why, Sheriff, that sounds like an immoral suggestion.'

'Don't it just.'

The twinkle in Digweed's brown eyes slowly turned to a more serious look in the long silence that followed. 'Sure, she came to my place,' he admitted.

'Matter of fact, she was with me most nights during the last three weeks, but not Saturday night.'

'Why not?'

'She told me Rex Neeson had made her an offer she felt she couldn't refuse. She was going to talk it over with him that night after the saloons were closed.'

'How did you feel about that, Harry?'

'I didn't like it. I warned her not to have anything to do with Neeson, but she wouldn't listen. She was sick of Moe Langley's rules and regulations and figured she'd have more freedom working for Neeson.'

'But you didn't want her working for him because you knew he fancied her himself, is that it? It would have meant no more visits to warm your bed, wouldn't it?'

Digweed ran a hand through his red hair, picked up his pipe and began stuffing the bowl with baccy.

'You were jealous, Harry, weren't you?'

'Sure I was, if you must know. I hate that man's guts. I knew if Jennie went to work for him that'd be the last I'd see of her. We had some good times, Jennie and me. Neeson and all his money!'

'I've allus had Neeson figured as a bit of a skin-flint. Was Jennie interested in money?'

'Who ain't? Only she never sold herself, if that's what you mean. I never gave her a cent and that's the truth. There was never any need for that.'

So it seemed that Josh Wragby's notion had been the right one, at least in part. Digweed was younger, but not all that much. Not a big man, but immensely strong and virile. Maybe he just had more of what Jennie wanted in a man, a more demanding and dominant attitude towards a woman. Maybe if Josh had been less of a gentleman . . . Gilpin was beginning to think Jennie Clark had been a nymphomaniac.

'Jennie was a good looking young woman, so I don't reckon you were the first man she'd gotten intimate with, do you?'

Digweed's eyes glinted angrily, as if the possibility was inconceivable, but he was intelligent enough to face reality and slowly he relaxed. He lowered his eyes, his pipe still unlit.

'I guess not,' he conceded after a long silence.

'But she never mentioned anybody, here in town, I mean?'

'No. I don't think there was anybody except me.'

Gilpin had no intention of disillusioning him. 'So you don't know who might have killed her?'

Digweed's mouth hardened as he replied, 'I wish I did. I'd put the rope around his neck myself.'

Moe Langley had obviously kept Jennie's Sacramento escapades to herself. Of one thing Gilpin was quite sure . . . the girl had learned the art of discretion as a result of those experiences, yet it was beginning to look as if her appraisal of men had not improved much. The sheriff formed the opinion that Harry Digweed had been genuinely fond of her.

But who else had known about her assignation with Rex Neeson?

Harry Digweed was well known for his fiery temper and jealousy is a powerful motive for murder.

SIX

Sheriff Gilpin strolled down the street as a quartet of riders headed towards him, with Walt Martin leading the way, a boy with fair hair poking out under his hat, about the age Martin had mentioned, alongside him. None of them were smiling, an indication that they were in town on serious business.

They dismounted outside a fine two-storey building that had a shingle swinging from the stoop on two chains, with the inscription

Eli Atkins
Attorney-at-law.

The woman was tall and lean, with red hair floating way below her shoulders. She pushed the broad-brimmed hat back off her head and followed Walt Martin to the door. Gilpin was near enough to catch the instruction she gave to her son as she turned to look at him.

'Watch the horses, Zeke. If I need you I'll call you.'

Her escort dismounted, removed his fawn hat and

48

sleeved his brow, revealing a head that had brown hair above his ears and at the back of his neck, but otherwise he was completely bald. He might once have been a handsome man, Gilpin judged, and when he smiled at the boy the sheriff could understand what Walt Martin had said about him having a lot of charm. Apart from a nose that was a little too big, his features were even and he had an engaging smile. A man who had taken good care of his teeth.

He was a big, powerful man. His hands were bigger than those of most men and it was possible he could be useful in a fist fight.

The Winchester rifle poking out of a saddle pouch and the Smith and Wesson 1870 American .44 Model revolver nestling at his right hip alerted the sheriff to the fact that this man was no stranger to firearms. Gilpin could well understand Walt Martin's concern. Maybe Idle was the kind of gunman who smiled at his victim just before he put a bullet into his belly. Martin, tall and powerful though he was himself, had good reason to be apprehensive if the situation went against the woman who called herself Laura Parker.

Gilpin halted in front of the big man. 'Howdy. Stranger in town, ain't you.'

The sheriff made it a statement, not a question.

The big man noticed the silver star, fashioned a wide smile and held out his hand. 'A pleasure to meet you, Sheriff. I'm Horace Idle and this here's Ezekiel Parker.'

'You're not related then.'

'No. I'm a friend of his mother's. I think you must

have known his father: a man by the name of Roger Talbot. I'm told he died in a fire here a year or so ago?'

'I knew Talbot. Didn't know he had a son though.' Gilpin offered the boy a smile, figuring he was the innocent pawn in what might be the biggest con he had ever come across. 'Howdy, son.'

'Hi, Sheriff. You gotta lotta notches on your gun?'

'County sheriffs don't cut notches on their guns, Ezekiel.'

'Oh. I thought all gunfighters did that.'

'But I'm not a gunfighter, Zeke, I'm a peace officer.'

'You mean you've never killed anybody?'

'I didn't say that. Sometimes we have to kill gunfighters an' outlaws to protect innocent citizens.'

'Oh. I see.'

'Hope you do. Where you from, Zeke?'

'San Francisco.'

'Then you've had a mighty long ride.'

'Sure have. It's taken us weeks to get here. That's why Uncle Horace came along, to make sure we got here safely.'

Horace Idle had already said the two were not related, so he was obviously an adopted "uncle", indicating that the man and the boy had formed a close friendship.

Gilpin pretended ignorance as he looked back at Idle. 'Where are you staying?'

The boy answered for him. 'Out at the ranch with Mr Martin.'

Eyebrows lifting under his mop of hair, the sheriff

said, 'Now ain't you the lucky ones. Good man, Mr Martin.'

Before either of them could respond Walt Martin came out and called to them. 'Ezekiel, Mr Idle, would you come inside, please. Mr Atkins wants to see you. Good morning, Sheriff. I'd like a word after I'm through in here.'

'I'll be in my office, Walt.'

Eli Atkins had felt the weight of responsibility for the property of the late Roger Talbot, as he had already explained to Laura Parker.

'Mr Talbot owned property here in town as well as the ranch, Mrs Parker, and although I've informed tenants of the buildings which were rented out, they are refusing to pay the rents, for a number of reasons.'

'Surely the law can compel them to do that, can't it?'

'The law does not operate here in Buzzards Creek as it might in San Francisco. For example, Mr Talbot had a ten per cent stake in the lumber yard, owned by Chetwyn Handley, but Chet claims that now Roger is dead, that percentage reverts to him.'

'On what grounds does he make this claim?'

'It was repayment for a loan, which Chet says has been repaid several times over, and George Taggart takes the same viewpoint.'

'Taggart?'

'The man who owns the livery stables. He had the same arrangement with Roger.'

'The way I see it, a ten per cent stake in any business is not automatically revoked by the death of the holder. That money should be set aside for the deceased's heir.'

'I do have sympathy with your viewpoint, Mrs Parker, and in law you are right, but there has to be a question about the rights of an illegitimate son. I'm afraid you'll have to pursue the claim on behalf of your son through the court. Perhaps we should have him in and explain the difficulties?'

Walt Martin had sat silently by throughout the discussion, but now he spoke up. 'I'll go get him.'

Laura Parker said, 'Ask Mr Idle to come in too, Mr Martin. I'd like him to know the situation.'

Now she was explaining the problems to Horace Idle, while Eli Atkins and Walt Martin waited, both of them wondering how much interest Idle could have in the claim being made on behalf of the thirteen years old boy.

Idle switched his gaze to Atkins. 'Now you listen to me, mister. That boy is entitled to inherit his father's property. As his lawyer it's your job to arrange it, so quit stallin' and get on with it.'

'I can't do that, Mr Idle. My own life could well be in danger if I tried it without the backing of the circuit judge.'

'Then you'd best get him behind you, hadn't you? Just who else is involved in Talbot's properties here in Buzzards Creek?'

'Ben Casey, for one. He has managed the biggest store in town for years, after Roger bailed him out when he hit money troubles. Ben built the original store himself and also claims his debts are cancelled by Roger's death.'

'I guess I'll have to pay this Casey a visit and straighten him out some. That's why I came along with Laura an' Zeke, to make sure they get what's rightfully theirs.'

'If you take my advice, Mr Idle, you'll achieve your objective far better by going through the due processes of the law. If the judge finds in favour of young master Parker here, there will be no problem.'

'And if he doesn't?'

'Then you will meet with considerable opposition.'

Idle looked towards Walt Martin. 'How about you, Mr Martin. You aim to be part of the opposition?'

'I will accept whatever ruling the court makes, Mr Idle.'

'You mean you're not gonna accept Zeke's claim without him and his mother havin' to go to court?'

'That is what I'm saying, I guess.'

'Well guess again, mister. As of today I'm takin' control of that ranch on behalf of young Zeke here. You can stay on as foreman while you teach me the ropes. After that. . . ?'

'You have no authority over me or the ranch, Mr Idle.'

'You wanna bet?'

The menace in his tone of voice sent shivers of alarm coursing through Martin's veins.

Eli Atkins was moved to protest. 'That attitude will

serve no good purpose, Mr Idle, either for you or Mrs Parker and her son.'

'Well you've gotten a straight alternative, Mr Lawyer. Just you get all the relevant papers drawn up and get the right signatures on 'em, then hand 'em over to Mrs Parker. Good day to you.' He turned towards the door. 'Let's go, Laura.'

Her eyes were cold as she stared back at Eli Atkins and in that stare he recognized an uncompromising resolution. The pleasant, attractive woman who had first faced him across his desk had turned into something almost unbelievably ruthless.

'I knew that man was trouble, Eli,' Martin said when the two men were left alone. 'I'd like you to come with me to see the sheriff and acquaint him with Idle's threats.'

'You go along, Walt. It would not do for me to be seen by Idle or Mrs Parker to be taking sides. If the sheriff wants confirmation of what you tell him, I'll be glad to back you up.'

'I knew that man was trouble as soon as he arrived at the ranch, Eli,' Martin repeated.

'I think you're right. All the more reason to tread softly. Play along with him for the time being. I'm sure Mrs Parker will see the wisdom of my advice after she's had time to consider.'

They left Zeke in charge of the horses outside Casey's Store. Laura Parker did not want her son to witness any unpleasantness which might transpire between

Ben Casey and her bodyguard. Casey smiled a welcome as the couple moved towards him. Neither of them returned his smile.

The woman said, 'Could we speak to you in private, Mr Casey? I take it you are Mr Ben Casey?'

'That's right, ma'am, but why would you want to talk with me in private?'

She flashed him her most engaging smile and he was captivated by the seductive pale green eyes.

'Come through to the parlour. We can talk there.'

They followed him and heard him ask his wife to watch the store for a while. She looked puzzled but did not argue.

Laura Parker introduced herself and Horace Idle, then she said, 'It is my understanding that you managed this store for Roger Talbot until he died, Mr Casey. Is that correct?'

'Begging your pardon, ma'am, but I don't think that is any of your business.'

Idle snarled, 'We're makin' it our business!'

'There is no need to be unpleasant, Mr Idle.' He looked back into those pale green eyes. 'May I ask what possible interest you could have in my store, Mrs Parker?'

'I am the mother of Roger's son. We are here to claim his inheritance.'

Considerably disturbed by this news, Casey blurted out, 'I never knew Talbot had a son.'

'Well you know now, Mr Casey, so I suggest we talk about how soon you can be ready to hand over the holding.'

'Hand over?' Casey stared back at her with amazement reflecting in his eyes. 'But this is *my* store. I built it, before Talbot ever came to Buzzards Creek.'

'But you ran into financial difficulties, didn't you, and. . . .'

'My financial affairs are my business and no one else's.'

She eyed him steadily, knowing she could outstare him, getting ready to make an accurate guess from what little Eli Atkins had said about Talbot having 'bailed out' Casey when he was in trouble. Eventually Casey's indignity disintegrated.

'Is it not a fact that Roger bought the store from you when you were in difficulties and then allowed you to stay on to run it for him, Mr Casey?'

'Who told you that?'

'Roger's lawyer, Mr Eli Atkins. We would be quite willing to allow you to continue in that capacity, if you so wish . . . after the papers are in our possession.'

Later he was to wonder where he had found the courage to make his protest, but his voice was strong as he bridled, 'This store belongs to me, not your son, Mrs Parker, so kindly leave at once. I will not be cheated a second time.'

'How can you be cheated out of what is not rightfully yours?'

'Get out! Both of you!'

Horace Idle took three steps forward and grabbed Casey by the shirt front, dwarfing the storekeeper as he pulled the Smith and Wesson revolver from its holster. He rammed the barrel under the fleshy part of Casey's jaw and said in a voice dripping with evil intent, 'You in a hurry to die, mister?'

Casey tried to speak but all that came from his throat was a croak as his startled eyes looked into Idle's.

'This store belongs to Ezekiel Parker, Roger Talbot's son, and startin' today, you put the takings into a bank account in his mother's name. She'll look after all his interests until he's old enough to do it himself. You get me?'

He released his grip on the storekeeper and clubbed him to the floor with the gun. Blood began to pour out of a head wound as Idle looked down on him.

'That's just a warnin'. This store ain't no good to a dead man, so remember, you open the account in the name of Laura Parker. Inform the bank teller she'll be in later to sign the necessary form, or whatever he needs. Good day, Casey.'

He turned and walked out, back through the store, to return to Ezekiel. Laura Parker lingered long enough to favour Ben Casey with that cold stare she had given Eli Atkins, then she, too, left.

Mrs Casey watched through the window as the visitors mounted their horses and moved off, then she went back into the living quarters. When she saw the blood running down her husband's face she let out a strangled cry of alarm.

SEVEN

Walt Martin had only just finished explaining what had transpired in Eli Atkins' sanctum when Ben Casey's wife burst into the Sheriff's Office. Both men stood up as the plea erupted from her mouth, large dark brown eyes staring even more than usual in her distress.

'Come quick, Sheriff. My husband has been attacked. He's bleeding!'

'Sounds like you need the doctor, Mrs Casey,' Gilpin told her.

'Will you go to my husband while I fetch the doctor?'

'I'll do that, right away, ma'am.'

She turned and hurried out again.

The two men eyed each other as Martin said, 'Now do you believe Idle has already shed the nice guy image? I'll come along with you, Sheriff.'

Ben Casey was sitting in an armchair, holding a piece of white linen to his head when they walked through the store to the living quarters. Blood had discoloured the cloth but the man appeared to be only superficially hurt.

58

'What happened, Ben?' Gilpin asked.

'Man and a woman came in and said they wanted to talk. Fed me some gush about this store now being owned by Roger Talbot's son. I told 'em straight it's mine and ordered them out. Then this feller hit me with his gun barrel. Knocked me senseless for a few seconds. Threatened to kill me if I didn't open an account at the bank for a Mrs Laura Parker – that was the woman – and deposit all my takings in it.'

'Feller by the name of Idle, was it?'

'That's him. Big man, with hands like hams. He scares me.'

'I'll have a word with him, Ben, but if I were you I'd consult Eli about your legal position. This woman may have the law on her side. You'd best be prepared for that.'

Anger flashed in the storekeeper's eyes. 'I built this store, Sheriff, and you know it! Nobody has a right to take it away from me.'

'The fact remains, Ben, that Talbot bought you out an' let you stay on to run it. This woman knows that, an' she's claimin' all Talbot's assets on behalf of her son. She says Talbot was the boy's father.'

'She's a fraud! Talbot never mentioned having a son.'

Walt Martin told him, 'She's gotten a birth certificate that names Roger Talbot as the boy's father, Ben.'

'Then it's a forgery! Are you gonna let this woman take the ranch away from you?'

'I'll leave that decision to the circuit judge, but

this Idle feller is a killer, Ben, and I'm no gunman.'

Casey looked hard at the sheriff. 'So what are you gonna do about him, Sheriff?'

'I can arrest him for breach o' the peace, Ben, but misdemeanour won't hold him for long. The problem won't go away unless you go through the court to make your claim stick. You win your case, then I can act if there's any more trouble.'

At that point Doc Rickman arrived to examine Casey's wound. Mrs Casey, eyes still staring, making her long nose seen yet more pronounced, hovered in agitation.

'You'll have a headache for a few hours, Ben, but you'll live,' Rickman diagnosed, noting the cut and the bump on the side of his head. 'I'll put some salve on it to ease the soreness.'

'Are you going to arrest that man, Sheriff?' Mrs Casey asked.

'If Ben lays a formal complaint I will, but as I've explained to him, it won't do a lotta good. Idle ain't gonna go away. I'll ride back to the ranch with Walt and give him a warnin'.'

'Warning!'

'If he ignores it an' causes more trouble, then I'll lock him up, Mrs Casey.'

'After he's killed me?' Casey queried with heavy sarcasm.

'Like I said, Ben, you'd best have words with Eli Atkins.'

Gilpin led the way back to the street, Walt Martin trailing him.

'They may not have returned to the ranch yet, Sheriff. Could be they've gone to see Bob Reid or Taggart.'

'Then let's find out.'

Horace Idle was waiting with Ezekiel Parker outside the saddler's shop when Sheriff Gilpin strolled along with Martin.

'You'd best stay out of this, Walt. You've gotten enough trouble of your own without gettin' involved with others.'

'I'll not get in your way, Sheriff.'

Gilpin did not need telling that the woman was inside, talking with Bob Reid. Neither did he need more than one guess as to why Idle had not gone inside with her. It was a safe bet that she did not want him roughing up the saddler in the same way he had Ben Casey.

Gilpin decided he could save himself a ride out to the ranch with Walt Martin.

'Mr Idle, I'd like . . .'

'Howdy again, Sheriff.' He was smiling amiably again, putting on the nice guy attitude.

'I've just had a complaint about you, so I'm warnin' you right now . . . you rough up another citizen in Buzzards Creek an' I'll throw you in jail. You understand me?'

The smile still in place, Idle said, 'Well now, Sheriff, you surely wouldn't want me to stand by while one of your citizens insults Mrs Parker and do nothing about it, would you?'

'I didn't hear nothin' about any insult.'

Idle shrugged. 'Would you have expected to? I take it that Casey feller is the one who made the complaint?'

'Actually it was his wife. We want no trouble, Idle.'

'If folks do the right thing, there'll be no trouble.'

'That's the point though. What you think is the right thing might not tally with what other folks think.'

Spreading his huge hands and pursing his lips in a gesture that indicated any trouble would not be of his making, Idle let the discussion drop.

As Gilpin went into the saddlery Walt Martin drew alongside Horace Idle, leading his horse. Idle looked at him.

Martin asked, 'You about ready to ride back to the ranch?'

'When Mrs Parker has finished her business.'

Inside, the red-haired woman was doing her best to charm the saddler with her bright eyes and seductive smile. Gilpin wondered if she'd practised it on Horace Idle and how much ice it would melt in Bob Reid. She turned to face him.

'Good-morning, Sheriff,' she greeted, seeing his badge. 'I'm Laura Parker.'

'Ma'am.' His gaze switched to Bob Reid. 'Everything all right, Bob?'

Reid was in no mood to discuss anything with the lawman. After their earlier wrangle, Gilpin was the last man he wanted to see, and he certainly did not want any further discussion in front of a stranger concerning his whereabouts at the time Jennie Clark was killed.

'I'm having a private conversation with Mrs Parker, Sheriff. Whatever it was you wanted to discuss, can it not wait?'

'Sure, Bob, sure. I'll leave you to it.'

Back outside he nodded to the boy and the two men who awaited Laura Parker's emergence from Reid's place, then ambled towards the livery stables. Taggart showed his surprise.

'Something you forgot, Sheriff?'

'No, George, I just came to warn you about possible trouble headin' your way.'

'Trouble? What kind of trouble?'

Gilpin explained about the arrival in town of Laura and Ezekiel Parker, accompanied by their bodyguard. He went on to reveal their mission and the attack on Ben Casey.

'So where do I come in?'

'They may know about that ten per cent stake you sold to Talbot when you were goin' through that bad patch a few years back.'

'But that was cancelled when Talbot died, Sheriff.'

'They may not see it that way, George. If they want to tackle you about it I reckon they'll be here pretty soon, so d'you want me to hang around in case there's an argument?'

Violence was something George Taggart had avoided for most of his life, but Gilpin knew he would not lie down and surrender at the first threat Horace Idle offered. It was obvious, however, that

Taggart did not want trouble.

'You mean this Idle feller might pistol-whip me if I don't agree to pay this woman and her son the old ten per cent?'

'It is possible, George.'

Taggart cogitated for well over a minute, realizing that to have the sheriff as a witness to any trouble would favour him.

'Why don't you potter around at the end stall, Sheriff, then you should be able to overhear any discussion.'

'Now that's a right sensible suggestion.'

It was less than ten minutes before the woman dismounted from her horse as George Taggart looked into her smiling face.

'You want to stable your horse, ma'am?' he asked her, his face a picture of innocence.

'You are Mr Taggart, the liveryman?'

'That I am. Never had no complaints, neither.

'I'll take your word for it, but I'm not staying in town for more than a few minutes. Could we talk?'

'Surely, ma'am. Come in out of the sun.'

Taggart led the way inside to a spot where the sheriff was unlikely to be seen, yet he would be able to hear what was said.

'What can I do for you, ma'am?'

Horace Idle had followed her into the stables, leaving the boy and Walt Martin to hang on to the reins of their horses.

'I'm Laura Parker and that young man you saw outside is my son. We've come to claim his inheritance.'

'Inheritance?' Taggart put on a puzzled expression. 'What has the boy's inheritance to do with me?'

'His father was Roger Talbot.'

'Oh, I see. That sly old fox. He never let on that he'd been married. I guess you married again, eh, you being Mrs Parker now?'

'My status is irrelevant, Mr Taggart. The point is that I understand Roger had a ten per cent stake in these stables and I was wondering what the position is at present.'

'Well now, ma'am, me and Mr Talbot had an understanding about some money he loaned me some years ago, but we both knew that arrangement would end on the death of either one of us.'

'Have you got anything in writing to prove that?'

'No, ma'am, it was a gentleman's agreement between the two of us. I built these stables when I first arrived here, years back. Ain't nobody gotten any entitlement but me.'

'Are you quite sure about that, Mr Taggart? I'd hate to think of my son being cheated out of what was rightfully his.'

Taggart laughed gently. 'Ma'am, if your boy is the rightful heir to Talbot's fortune he wouldn't give this place or my arrangement with his daddy a single thought. It barely makes a living for me, never mind about paying out a small percentage. Not even worth your while to pursue it in a court of law.'

'You may be right, Mr Taggart, but if I find out you're lying, I'll be back. Good day to you.'

'And to you.'

Horace Idle pushed a hard stare at Taggart before he followed the woman outside again. He watched them mount their horses. She did not look back as she urged her horse forward, swinging round to ride in the direction of the former Talbot ranch. The other three followed without a backward glance.

The sheriff came out of hiding and stood beside Taggart.

'What you think, Sheriff?'

'I think that woman warned Idle not t' beat up any more men in Buzzards Creek for the time bein', George.'

'You think she didn't believe me?'

Gilpin scratched his bearded chin. 'I don't think she did. I reckon she'll do some ferretin' an' be back, an' if you don't play ball, her hard man'll offer you a deal you night find hard to refuse.'

'He don't scare me none, and I've no intention of paying that woman a single cent. All deals ended when Talbot died.'

'I hope you're right, because if you ain't, there'll be a few busted heads around here afore much longer.'

Gilpin walked away, curiosity about what had transpired between Laura Parker and Bob Reid eating away inside him. Somehow he'd have to find out.

EIGHT

What with investigations into the brutal murder of Jennie Clark and the stir Laura Parker and her hard man had created in town, Gilpin had completely forgotten about 'Doc' Holliday, but as his belly began to rumble and remind him it was time he went for some lunch, he remembered that John Henry seldom got out of bed before noon. Time for Gilpin to call in on Eli Atkins and ferret out the legal implications of what was beginning to gather momentum around him, before seeking out his old friend.

Eli had a client with him and Gilpin was obliged to exercise patience for ten minutes, then the lawyer inquired what the sheriff wanted. The two men were not exactly friendly and Gilpin's reception was cool. As for the sheriff, he had little time for men who helped the likes of Roger Talbot to subjugate honest citizens for his own personal gain. Not that the sheriff had any reason to think Atkins had ever flouted the law, but he was convinced Eli used it for the maximum benefit of his clients.

'To what do I owe the pleasure, Sheriff?'

'This Parker woman . . .'

'What about her?'

'Seems she's likely to stir up a hornets' nest. You think she has a genuine claim on behalf of that boy?'

'A lawyer's knowledge of his client is privileged information, Sheriff, and I should not need to remind you of that fact.'

'But Laura Parker ain't your client, is she, Eli?'

Atkins was clearly irritated by the challenge but the sheriff continued to smile at him, anxious to avoid further friction.

'The fact that she is likely to become so and has already consulted me on the legal position of her son makes anything she said within the walls of this office confidential.'

'I wouldn't want you t'break any confidences, Eli, but that man she's brought along to protect her interests has already assaulted one of our citizens. Are you gonna condone that?'

'Certainly not. I abhor violence, as you should know.'

Gilpin did not know any such thing, convinced that Atkins had often turned a blind eye to skulduggery when it suited him.

'Then let's be practical. Did that woman say she had ever been married to Talbot?'

'No, she didn't make that claim.'

'So if Talbot really was the boy's father, he's likely t'be illegitimate?'

'There is that possibility,' Atkins conceded cautiously.

'An' the way I understand the law of inheritance, that would rule him out of any legal claim to property formerly owned by the late Roger Talbot.'

'It might, but Mrs Parker could challenge that assumption with a legal action.'

Gilpin fashioned another thin smile. 'I get the impression she ain't in favour o' goin' t'law, Eli. That Horace Idle is a hard man an' the tactic seems t'be the same as Talbot hinself used when he was rulin' the roost around here.'

'And precisely what is that?'

'Fear, Eli, fear. Toe the line or get a bullet in the belly. Idle threatened t'kill Ben Casey if he didn't put all his future takin's into a bank account in the name o' Laura Parker.'

Atkins seemed a little put out by the news. 'I was not aware of that, Sheriff.'

'That's why I'm tellin' you. That woman spells trouble.'

The silence hung like a thunder cloud in the enclosed space, making the room seem claustrophobic to the lawyer. When he made no comment, Gilpin went on.

'I'd like us t'work t'gether on this, Eli. I need t'know if Ben Casey has any real claim to ownership o' that store.'

'I warned Casey a year ago that he had better prepare himself in case any heir came along to make a claim for Roger's assets. As far as I know he has been banking his takings and using only what Talbot normally paid him to manage the store. At least I hope for his sake that is the case.'

'You mean if nobody had turned up t'make a claim, Ben could've reclaimed the business as his own?'

Atkins shrugged. 'It's just possible, bearing in mind that he himself built the original store, but legally he has a very thin case.'

'An' what about the rent Bob Reid was payin' for his place?'

'As Reid is a client of mine I cannot discuss that question with you.'

Gilpin rubbed his bearded chin thoughtfully. 'You mean Reid has been payin' you the rent all this time?'

'I can neither confirm nor deny that assumption.'

'Well . . . I can ask him myself.'

'That is your privilege.'

'An' smaller interests, like the ten per cent stake Talbot had in one or two other businesses here in town, how about them?'

Atkins leaned forward. 'I think it's past my lunchtime, Sheriff, if you will excuse me?'

Gilpin ignored the request. 'What about the ranch? Does Walt Martin have a legal right t'that?'

'I've given you all the help I can, Sheriff. Now if. . .?'

'I know, I know,' Gilpin's right hand fluttered in acceptance, 'it's way past your lunchtime. Thanks anyway, Eli. I'm obliged.'

'Glad to have been able to help. I'll show you out.'

'No need. I can find my way to the front door.'

*

John Henry Holliday was just being served with ante-
lope steaks and buckwheat cakes when Sheriff Gilpin
ambled towards his table in the hotel dining-room.
Business at the hostelry was a little slack and 'Doc'
had a table to himself.

'You want to join me, Jeff?'

'I'd kinda like that, John.'

Holliday gave the order for the sheriff to be served
and then invited him to help himself to coffee. 'Take
my cup, I've not used it yet. I'll get the woman to
bring me another.'

Gilpin was glad of the beverage. 'Thanks, John.
Seems like I've been doin' nothin' but yack all
mornin'. My mouth feels like it's full o' sawdust.'

'Made any progress with your woman murder?'

'I've gotten me a real good suspect, with no sound
alibi, but there ain't a cat-in-hell's chance o' provin'
it.'

'Is it just a hunch, or do you really think he did it?'

'I don't *want* t'think he did it, but I reckon he had
both motive and opportunity.'

'Not enough to arrest him though?'

'Not nearly enough, John. Not nearly enough.
What's more, he's a real nice feller, but even nice
fellers can kill if they get worked up enough, an' this
one does have a short fuse.'

'What's the motive?'

'Jealousy.'

Holliday shrugged. 'One of the most potent of

motives. I've often felt like strangling "Big Nose" Kate, I don't mind telling you, Jeff. That woman can be a right pain at times.'

'I did hear you two had gotten married.'

Holliday laughed sardonically. 'Nothing but rumour, Jeff.'

'Doc' had already started on his meal and when the sheriff's plate arrived the two men lapsed into silence and concentrated on eating. Afterwards they talked of old times, until Gilpin asked Holliday how long he intended staying in Buzzards Creek.

'Haven't decided yet. A few days, at least. I'm a mite tired, Jeff, and this seems like a restful place.'

'Don't count on it. There's trouble brewin' an' no mistake.'

'You need any help, old friend?'

'I might, but if you don't mind me sayin' so, I reckon you should be thinkin' of yourself an' go an' see Doc Rickman. He might be able t'give you sonethin' for that cough. Mebbe you're used to it, but it sounds right bad t'me.'

Even while Gilpin was speaking another bout of coughing had Holliday in its grip. When it passed he said hoarsely, 'I don't think he'll be able to help, Jeff, but lead me to him. I'll try anything once.'

NINE

Laura Parker had decided before she left San Francisco with her son and Horace Idle that she wanted to claim the late Roger Talbot's assets for Ezekiel with as little fuss as possible, but she was no fool. In law she knew it would be difficult to prove even that the boy had been sired by Talbot and harder still to claim what she felt was rightfully her son's inheritance. A son born out of wedlock had few rights in law. That was why she had enlisted the aid of Horace Idle. She had promised him rich pickings if he would squash any opposition. That he was capable she had no doubt. Idle was the hardest, most ruthless man she had ever met. He had wanted her body as well and, on those occasions when her own female desires had plagued her, she submitted to him. He had an insatiable sexual appetite and thrilled her like no man ever had before, including the father of her son. He was also a man of understanding and when she was not keen to satisfy him he was content to find his pleasures elsewhere. It therefore came as no surprise when he announced he was riding into town that night. He had no need to offer her an excuse.

Ezekiel was fascinated by his introduction to ranch life, keen to learn as much as he could as quickly as possible. His mother allowed him to fraternize with the ranch hands, leaving her to try and cement some kind of relationship with Walt Martin, the ranch manager. After supper, with Horace Idle riding to Buzzards Creek, she joined Martin out on the porch as he smoked his pipe and watched the sun sink lower in the sky, Ezekiel squatted outside the bunkhouse with the men, talking and listening in turn.

The silence between the red-haired woman and the prematurely grey-haired man had stretched to the point of becoming uncomfortable. Walt Martin decided to break it by getting nosy.

'How did you and Mr Talbot meet, Mrs Parker?'

'He owned a saloon in San Francisco. I was one of the girls he employed to entice the customers to spend their hard-earned cash.'

Martin wondered to what lengths she had gone to do that, but decided to be charitable. 'Getting them to buy you drinks that weren't worth the money, you mean?'

'The men knew that, Mr Martin, but I was young and pretty in those days and men have always been attracted by a pretty face.'

Not so young now, Martin decided, but still one helluva woman. As he had already found out, she could be a most charming and attractive woman, with a body that would still drive some men wild. He had also seen the hard glint that came into her eyes when she thought she might not be getting her own way.

'And you and Talbot became lovers.'

'Yes. He was a very attractive man and as I said, I was young enough to believe all his promises. It was when he sold the saloon and left Frisco without mentioning it to me that I had to face reality. His disappearance changed me, Mr Martin. I was expecting his child and I had no idea where he had gone. I had to learn to fend for myself. That once trusting young woman became a tough cookie. No man has walked all over me since then.'

'Not even Horace Idle?'

'Horace is in my employ, Mr Martin, nothing more,' she lied easily, having warned Idle days ago that there was to be no undue show of intimacy while they were at the ranch.

'He's a hard man, Mrs Parker.'

'Yes, Mr Martin, he is, and if I were a man I'd hate to cross him. The next man he kills won't be the first.'

Martin knew the statement was intended as a warning. 'I had worked that out for myself,' he said.

'I hope we can work things out, Walt. I may call you Walt?'

'Somehow I didn't think you wanted to be that friendly.'

She favoured him with her most disarming smile. 'Whatever have I done to give you that impression? When we get things settled, I want you to stay on as ranch manager.'

His head turned to face her, surprised by the statement. 'And what about Mr Idle? Are you saying he does not really want me to teach him the ropes, as he put it?'

'In spite of what he said this morning, as far as I am aware, he knows nothing about ranching, and I do know he is more at home in a saloon than he would be out here on the range.'

'That I can believe.'

'So you'll stay on?'

Their eyes held while he contemplated a future without the position he had occupied very agreeably for several years. 'If the law supports your claim to Mr Talbot's property, then I will consider your offer, Mrs Parker.'

'You don't think you would like working for a woman? Is that what troubles you?'

'How can I tell? I've never done it before.'

Her voice softly enticing, she said, 'I will need someone to keep the ranch going until Zeke is old enough to look after it for himself, so who better than the man who is already doing it?'

He could see the wisdom of that and he felt a grudging respect for her business acumen.

'If I may use a well-worn phrase, Mrs Parker, you're more than just a pretty face.'

All her life she had cherished admiration and she knew it would be to her advantage to keep on the good side of this man. 'You really find me attractive still, Walt?'

'I think you could charm Satan himself, Mrs Parker.'

Horace Idle was no mug when it came to playing poker and he increased his roll by some forty-seven dollars before deciding he was woman-hungry. He had already chosen the one he wanted to play with and, as she led him up the stairs to her room in The Four Aces, he was well aware that their ascent was being observed by the county sheriff. He was in no hurry to tangle with the lawman, yet he knew it was more than likely that he would have to kill him before many days had passed.

Watching him, Jeff Gilpin was having like-minded speculation. He didn't think Idle would go away quietly just because his methods of enforcing his will on the citizens of Buzzards Creek met with opposition. Idle would kill if he had to, just to let other men know he meant business. He would then resist any attempt Gilpin made to arrest him. Bullets would fly and one or both of them would die. Gilpin wondered just how good Idle was with a gun.

George Taggart was a peace-loving man and had seldom been provoked into violent action, but if the Parker woman tried to take ten per cent of his earnings he would cut up rough, no matter what Horace Idle threatened.

Bob Reid would likely pay the rent on his place rather than face up to violence, but Ben Casey was a different proposition. Roger Talbot's money had saved him from going bust and having to leave town and seek employment elsewhere in the old days, but it was Ben's hard work that had made the store prosper and Gilpin could picture him loading a shotgun the next time Horace Idle visited the store. He was hardly likely to meekly submit to another pistol whipping. Gilpin shuddered inwardly at what might happen to Ben and his family in such an event.

Chet Handley, the lumber merchant, was another who had sold ten per cent of his business to Roger Talbot at a time when he had needed cash money. Would he honour that contract for the benefit of a thirteen-year-old boy whose mother claimed he was Talbot's son? Eli Atkins would have a copy of that contract and, according to what Walt Martin had related, had already as good as admitted that much to Laura Parker.

The sheriff had already chewed over these facts with John Henry Holliday and the 'Doc' had offered his help if trouble stirred.

'It's not your problem, John. You're not paid t'keep the peace hereabouts. I am.'

Now, with the murders of two women still unsolved, Gilpin decided he'd had enough worries for one day. Tomorrow something might break in his favour, though he was not exactly optimistic about it.

He headed for the street and the comfort of his bed.

TEN

Chetwyn Handley was a worried man. He was going over in his mind the conversation he'd had with George Taggart over a glass of beer the night before.

'You get visitors today, Chet?'

'Visitors?'

'Yeah. Woman by the nane of Laura Parker and a big feller she called Horace Idle. Her bodyguard, seemed like.'

'No, I ain't seen 'em.'

'I reckon you will. Can't think how they come to miss you.'

Handley looked puzzled. 'Tell me about it.'

'Well . . . seems like this woman has a thirteen-year-old son. She reckons Roger Talbot was his father and they're here to claim all Talbot's assets on behalf of the boy. They seem well informed about the deals we had with Talbot before he died and they reckon on laying their hands on the ten per cent stake Talbot had with all of us, so I reckon that includes you.'

A worried frown creased Handley's brow. 'I thought all that was finished with after Talbot got himself killed.'

'So did I, only they don't see it that way. I reckon they got their information from Atkins.'

'Eli should've kept his fat mouth shut.'

'That's what I think, but the damage is done, I reckon.'

'What you aim to do about it, George?'

'I ain't paying that woman a red cent, only the sheriff reckons that Idle feller she has in tow can get real nasty. Seems like he beat up Ben Casey when he told 'em to get lost.'

'So what did Gilpin do about that?'

'Warned him off, but that's about all, from what I hear.'

'And you think he'll be taking a crack at me if I don't play ball, is that it?'

Taggart contemplated his near empty glass before raising his eyes again and asking, 'What will you do, Chet?'

'I dunno. Reckon I'll have to consult Eli on the legal situation. If this boy has a genuine claim, don't see what we can do about it.'

'Well you please yourself, Chet, but I've paid out enough for the money Talbot let me have.'

A law-abiding citizen, Chet Handley had no wish to start giving a percentage of his profits to this Parker woman on behalf of her son, but if the lad had a legal right. . .?

It was around ten o'clock that morning when Laura Parker rode into the yard with her young son and

Horace Idle. She introduced herself and Ezekiel, then looked around her.

'Quite a business you're running here, Mr Handley.'

Handley shrugged. 'It has its ups and downs, ma'am. What can I do for you?'

She explained her mission, then said, 'Will you accept the right of my son to claim the ten per cent stake his father had in your timber yard, Mr Handley?'

Handley rubbed his chin thoughtfully. 'I'm a law-abiding citizen, ma'am, so I reckon we'd best go talk this thing over with Mr Attins, don't you?'

'I do hope you're not going to be difficult about it.'

'Not if your claim is legal, ma'am, no. The way I see it, the percentage Roger held was cancelled after he was killed, but if I'm wrong. . .?'

Handley spread his hands and shrugged in resignation. Idle spoke up for the first time. 'You're wrong all right, mister, and you'd best play ball or somebody might just drop a lighted match in some of those shavings over there while you're tucked up in bed one night.'

Handley gave him a hard stare and challenged firmly, 'I didn't catch your name.'

'His name is Idle, Mr Handley,' Laura Parker interposed, 'but don't let that fool you. He can become very active when it suits him.'

'You mean if I don't agree right away he'll pistol-whip me the same as he did Ben Casey?'

'I see no need for violence, Mr Handley.'

'Well maybe you should point out to Mr Idle that a ten per interest in a burnt-out timber yard pays no dividends, ma'am.'

She turned her eyes on Idle and said, 'I don't think we shall be having any trouble with Mr Handley, Horace, so why don't we do as he suggested and go get this little matter settled in the lawyer's office?'

Idle's shoulders lifted and fell. 'You're the boss.'

'Well now lookee here, boys,' Grover Nichols drawled, 'if it ain't that there sheriff who killed Rube.'

Sheriff Gilpin's eyes lifted to gaze into the outlaw's smilingly sardonic face. He found himself looking into an armoury of six guns held by the outlaw gang he had vanquished only two days before. They were still sitting quietly astride their horses, but every one of those guns was pointing his way.

'I told you we'd be back, Sheriff, when you didn't have that Holliday to side you.'

Gilpin's belly felt like an empty pit as he looked into the snouts of those fisted guns, but he fashioned a thin smile of defiance. 'That you did, an' I recall I said I'd be waitin' for you.' He scrubbed a hand through his beard. 'Trouble is I didn't figure you'd be back quite so soon.'

How in hell was he going to get out of this? he asked himself. I might get one or two of 'em afore they get me, but I'll still end up dead. He cursed himself for having been so preoccupied with the problems of finding enough evidence to convict a murderer and the hassle he knew would soon come from Laura Parker and Horace Idle. Without these latest problems concentrating his mind he would have been more aware of what was going on around him.

'Well now, Sheriff, one of us had hear'ered that Holliday don't git outa bed afore noon, so we figured he wouldn't be around to butt in at this time o' day. Looks like we were right, don't it?'

They were, but having it thrust down his throat did not make Gilpin feel any easier. He'd been a dumb fool and now he was about to pay the price.

He didn't know why he should put his trust in God, but if he could keep Grover Nichols talking long enough a miracle might just come to his rescue.

'I guess you're smarter'n I figured, Nichols.'

'Which jest goes t'show what a dumb fool you are, jest like most sheriffs, I reckon. You gotten any last requests afore we blow you t'hell?'

Gilpin appeared to cogitate, knowing he was going to have to make his play at any moment. Every second was precious to a man staring death in the face.

'You mean,' he said slowly, 'you'd grant a dumb sheriff his last request?'

Grover Nichols shrugged. 'Well now, Sheriff, I ain't usually a generous man, but I reckon I can afford t'be in your case. You ain't gotten above a minute t'live.'

Where the hell is everybody? Gilpin asked himself. Probably ducking out of the line of fire if any men were around in the sidestreet that led up to Chet Handley's timber yard. 'Don't allow much time for my request then, does it?'

A broad grin stretched Grover Nichols' mouth. 'Whaddaya have in mind, Sheriff?'

'I'd like t'take you with me!'

As he spat the words out Gilpin's right hand closed over the butt of his gun and he threw himself to the ground, rolling rapidly, loosing off a shot every time his eyes were looking up at the mounted outlaws. He saw them falling from their saddles and from somewhere behind him he was vaguely aware of exploding cordite and the whine of rifle bullets. Not until his gun was empty and every one of the six outlaws lay dead in the dust did he realize there was a burning sensation in his left leg and that his foot felt numb. He heard running feet growing louder as he looked down and saw the hole in his left boot. Even then it did not register that he had lost his big toe.

'You hurt bad, Sheriff?'

Gilpin raised his head to see Horace Idle looking down on him, with other men crowding round with anxious and curious expressions on their faces.

'Was that you helpin' out?' he queried as he struggled to his feet and tried to stand normally.

Idle grabbed hold of him as he stumbled due to the numbness in his foot. 'No, it wasn't me. I just heard the shooting.'

'Well somebody must've been backin' me up, or

I'd be dead now.'

Idle looked around at the bodies lying in the street and knew what he meant. 'I guess that's so. One man up against six would never have survived.' He looked down at the hole in Gilpin's left boot and said, 'I've heard of a man shooting himself in the foot but I reckon you've gotten off lightly, Sheriff.'

'You think I was dumb enough t'do that m'self?'

'No, I reckon it was a freak of aim. Probably your head was the target but none of those men could shoot straight. Looks like you've been hit in the thigh, too. That's blood on your pants.'

Gilpin looked down and saw that Idle was right.

'I'll help you to the doc's surgery,' Idle offered. 'You'll have to hobble some. Just put your arm around my shoulder.'

Now what game is he playing, trying to get into my good books? After what had happened to Ben Casey, Gilpin was not about to believe that Horace Idle had become an angel of mercy all of a sudden.

He did not hear Josh Wragby say to the men around him, 'We'd best make sure these men *are* all dead, fellers.'

ELEVEN

'What's that rifle doing there, Harry?'

Harry Digweed found he could not meet his employer's gaze as he replied, 'I figured you might need some protection, boss.'

'Protection?' Chet Handley queried.

'From that feller who came with the Parker woman. I heard last night what he'd done to Ben Casey.'

Handley was considerably moved by Digweed's concern for his safety, but puzzled, too. He had never known Harry to go out shooting. Then something clicked in his brainbox.

'How come you knew they would be coming?'

'A little bird told me it was likely.'

It was not hard to put a name to the little bird. 'And would that little bird have its nest down at the livery?'

'Aw, boss, what difference does it make?'

Handley glanced at the rifle again, propped up against the wall. 'So it was you who backed up the sheriff while I was away to Eli Atkins' office?'

Digweed lifted his head and grinned. 'Allus pays to keep on the good side o' the law, boss.'

'Does Gilpin know?'

'I doubt it. I slipped back here once we'd killed them fellers. Just lucky I happened to see them ride into town and recalled seeing them ride out after the sheriff killed their leader on Sunday afternoon.'

'And you figured they'd come back to get even?'

'I did hear one o' them had threatened to do just that, so it didn't take much working out.'

'Lucky for Gilpin then. Not even he could've survived the guns of six killers. I hear he's gotten away with a superficial flesh wound in his left leg and lost the big toe off his left foot.'

'You don't reckon he'll mind having a limp then?'

'Wouldn't you rather have a limp than a pine box, Harry?'

'Reckon so.'

Handley's gaze lingered on his assistant for a few more seconds, then he said, 'Take the rest of the day off, Harry. After what you've done you deserve it. I'll pay you for the full day.'

The wiry, red-haired Digweed grinned appreciatively. 'Thanks, boss, but I wouldn't know what to do with it. Best if I carry on.'

'Suit yourself. Time for a bite to eat, anyway.'

Handley walked away, knowing that Digweed had felt the isolation of living alone after his wife had died, yet there was a frown of bemusement on his forehead. How long had Harry been in possession of a rifle and what had he wanted it for?

John Henry Holliday, freshly shaved and immaculately dressed, visited the sheriff after he'd had his customary late breakfast. It was close to three o'clock.

'I hear you almost got yourself killed this morning, Jeff.'

Gilpin put on a smile. 'I was prayin' for a miracle, John, an' I got one. Somebody was backin' me up with a rifle, so I guess it wasn't you.'

'I wouldn't know what to do with a rifle, as you well know. The handgun and the knife have always served me well.'

The sheriff had heard tales of how handy and ruthless Holliday had been with the blade, although he had no first hand experience of it. Back in the days when they had become friends the 'Doc' had always seemed such a mild-mannered gambling man, although even then Gilpin had heard the rumours.

'Well I hope that knife stays in its sheath while you're here in Buzzards Creek, John.'

Holliday knew what he meant. He wouldn't want to have to kill his old friend if he tried to arrest him for slitting the throat of some obnoxious character who tried to make a name for himself at Holliday's expense.

'Reckon I made a mistake about Buzzards Creek. It ain't the nice quiet town I'd been led to believe. Almost got yourself killed by that Talbot feller back awhile, and now some good citizen with a rifle saves your hide again. Losing a toe is better than getting yourself killed, only you'll be no use with a gun if any more trouble breaks out, hobbling around on crutches.'

'You volunteerin' to be sworn in as my deputy?'

Holliday grunted in disgust. 'I'd rather go back to pulling teeth!'

'Done much of that lately?'

'Hell, no. Having to look into other men's mouths is a disgusting way to make a living. Give me the cards any time.'

A small silence developed between them, until Gilpin asked, 'You didn't happen t'hear who was usin' that rifle, did you?'

'No, I didn't. Seems like he vanished into thin air.'

'Forget what I said about prayin' for a miracle, John. You don't believe in 'em an' neither do I.'

'I'll keep my ears open. Somebody might know.'

'Whoever he was, he's one helluva marksman.'

'How many of those jaspers do you think you killed yourself?'

'Two at the most. I was rollin' an' shootin' at the same time, but without that man with the rifle t'take out the others, one of 'em would've gotten me.'

How much longer could Jeff Gilpin's luck last? Holliday asked himself.

Not long after supper Chetwyn Handley called in to see the sheriff.

'How are you feeling, Jeff?'

'My temper ain't too good. What use is a sheriff on

crutches?'

'Seems like you need a deputy again.'

'Well Conway is long gone an' so is Joe Blondell.'

'How about Harry Digweed?'

Gilpin shot forward in his chair, astonishment in his hard stare. 'Harry!'

'Harry. Didn't you know it was him who saved your life this morning?'

'I don't believe it!'

Handley's face was wreathed in a big smile, revealing his delight in being able to astound the normally cool-headed lawman. As for Gilpin, not only was he finding it hard to accept that Harry Digweed had been his saviour, but he knew he didn't want to believe it, either. Digweed was his prime suspect for the murder of Jennie Clark.

'You want I should ask him to come and see you?'

The sheriff considered the suggestion carefully before answering. 'If you could get him to call in without letting him know I want to see him, I reckon I'd like the chance to thank him.'

'I'll think of something. You take it easy now.'

The visitors came in a steady stream that evening, all anxious to hear first hand what had happened during the morning shootout, while Gilpin inwardly fretted and fumed because Harry Digweed was not one of them. He had almost given up hope when, well after ten o'clock, Digweed knocked on his door and entered.

'Hello, Harry. What can I do for you?'

'Why, nothing, Sheriff. I was just on my way home and thought I'd like to see how you were coping. They tell me you lost a big toe.'

'That's so, Harry. Surprisin' how you miss a little thing like that when it ain't there no more.'

Digweed grunted something unintelligible.

Gilpin said, 'Where did you learn t'shoot like that, Harry?'

Shaken by the sudden question, Digweed found hinself tongue-tied. The sheriff held his gaze until the lumber man cottoned on.

'That Chet Handley is getting a big mouth.'

'I guess I owe you, Harry, but I still wanna know why you had that rifle an' where you learned t'use it.'

'I was in the Cavalry for three years. Got me court-marshalled for telling an officer just what I thought of him. You can guess the rest.'

'An' you kept quiet about it all these years.'

'Ain't nothing to boast about, is it?'

'The way you handle a rifle is.'

Digweed shrugged. 'It's like riding a horse, I guess. Once you've learned how you never forget.'

Even if I ever gather enough evidence, how the hell can I arrest a man when, had it not been for him, I'd be dead? Gilpin grumbled silently. Reluctantly he was obliged to admit that any man who could kill as ruthlessly as Digweed had that morning was the most likely deputy he would find in Buzzards Creek.

He took a deep breath. 'Harry, I've gotten me a problem. You feel like helpin' me out?'

'Anything I can do, Sheriff,' Digweed offered without hesitation.

'I'm expectin' trouble from that Idle feller. Y'know, the one this Laura Parker has in tow. As you can see, I'm gonna be laid up, for a few days. How about pinnin' on a deputy's badge?'

Digweed's voice was full of disbelief. 'Me!?'

'You, Harry. You can ride an' you can shoot. When word gets around that you killed at least four o' them jaspers this mornin', folks'll respect you. Even Horace Idle.'

TWELVE

After breakfast Walt Martin rode off with the men to inspect the fence repairs they had been working on and to assess how many cattle would be available for the Fall sale, thankful for the opportunity to get away from Laura Parker and her shadow. Around Horace Idle he still felt uncomfortable after the man's threats two days ago.

Idle himself was too concerned about what had transpired between the woman and Eli Atkins the day before to take any interest in what the ranch manager was doing. With Martin and Laura talking together for most of the previous afternoon and evening there had been no opportunity to ask her. Now, Martin having agreed to take Ezekiel along, he took his chance.

'So what happened in that lawyer's office yesterday, Laura?'

'As he said before we left you outside, Mr Handley is resigned to Ezekiel claiming the ten per cent stake in his business, given certain conditions.'

'And they are?'

'That I can prove Ezekiel really is Roger Talbot's son and that he would have wanted . . .'

Idle cut in. 'But you've gotten that certificate.'

She smiled at him indulgently. 'Because I stated to the Registrar that Talbot was his father does nothing to prove it. Many a woman has made similar claims and some have proved false.'

'So what does that mean?'

'It means Eli Atkins and the men we are making claims on can challenge those claims in the court-room.'

'So you want me to lean on them a bit, huh? Make them see some sense?'

She shook her head. 'I've decided we should try persuasion rather than confrontation first, Horace. I did point out yesterday that Ezekiel bears his father's facial features, and that seemed to have some effect, at least with the lawyer.'

He sensed her unease. 'But?'

Her eyes were troubled as she looked back at him. 'I can't prove that Roger even knew anything about the boy's existence. Then there is the fact that Ezekiel is . . .'

He cut in on her hesitation. 'A bastard?'

'Don't call him that! He is my son!'

The heavy shoulders rose and fell again. 'Illegitimate?'

'Illegitimate, yes. The big question is whether or not an illegitimate child can inherit his father's property?'

'So we have to persuade them he can, you mean?'

'Yes, Horace, we do, but I don't want you roughing up or killing any of them just yet.'

He smiled and it was a pleasant smile; the smile that had first drawn her attention to him. 'And have you decided what my reward is going to be?'

'You've already had me, Horace.'

He leaned towards her. 'But not lately, Laura. Now the boy is out of the way and all the ranch hands gone, we've gotten an hour or two to pleasure ourselves.'

'You knew my father well, didn't you, Mr Martin?'

'Yes, Zeke, I did. As well as most folks, I suppose.'

They were riding at a walk, with Martin doing a mental count of the stock ready for market.

'What was he like?'

'He was a tall, fine looking man. I didn't see a lot of him, because he lived in town, not out at the ranch. He trusted me to look after it for him and make sure we made a profit.'

'And did you? Make a profit, I mean.'

'Every year, Zeke.'

At first Martin had addressed the boy by his full Christian name, but Ezekiel had made it clear he preferred to be called by the abbreviation.

'Was he a nice man?'

'He was always very fair with me, but there were people in town who did not like him.'

'Why was that?'

'Oh . . . some because he was wealthy. He owned a saloon in town and properties he rented out to townsfolk. Then there were business rivals. Money does things to people, Zeke. My advice to you would be not to let yourself be ruled by money. The Good Book tells us that the love of money is the root of all evil and I think that is right.'

'You mean it's wrong to have money?'

'No, no, Zeke, I don't mean that. It's making money your God instead of the Almighty that is wrong.'

'I see what you mean.'

Martin favoured the boy with a smile, seeing no sense in telling him that his father *had* made money his god. 'Then you're smarter than most.'

There was nothing to be gained by being nasty to the boy. Martin knew Ezekiel was just the pawn in a power struggle that could end up getting very nasty if the likes of Chetwyn Handley, Ben Casey and George Taggart dug their heels in. He liked this son of Roger Talbot and he could see there was a facial and physical resemblance to his father. For an only child he was remarkably placid and unspoiled. Whatever Laura Parker might have been or had become, she had raised her son to respect his elders and be polite to everyone.

Martin knew he never had any legal right to claim the ranch as his own and he was resigned to being responsible to whoever did have that right, or even to being dismissed and forced to search for fresh employment. Positions such as his were not readily available any more. He had already half decided to continue as ranch manager on behalf of the boy once the problems with Eli Atkins had been resolved, but he intended to make it quite clear to Laura Parker that staying on would be dependent on her keeping Horace Idle in his place.

'Will you teach me all about cattle ranching, Mr Martin?'

'Sure I will. Now the first thing you need to know . . .'

Doc Rickman arrived early to take a look at the sheriff's wounded foot, knowing the lawman would be having some pain where the missing digit had left a nasty mess. He was glad to see that Gilpin had been sensible and not aggravated the wound and caused it to bleed again.

'It's nice and clean, Sheriff. I'll give you something to take the edge off the pain. It will settle down in a day or two. Soon have you on your feet again, glaring at everybody.'

'I only glare at folks who irritate me, Doc, so if you wanna stay in my good books you'd best stop bein' facetious.'

Rickman smiled to himself. 'How's the leg wound?'

'You're the doctor; you take a look at it an' tell me.'

Rickman removed the bandage and saw the wound was clean. 'Just fine, Sheriff, just fine. I'll put a fresh dressing on it.'

Harry Digweed arrived soon after the medic had

departed.

'Any orders, Sheriff?'

'First thing you do is pin a badge on your vest. I take it Chet has given you indefinite leave from the wood yard?'

The new deputy smiled. 'And promised to keep the job open for me. He even told me it was his idea you should ask me to pin on this badge.'

'Matter of fact, he did. I thought he'd gone loco at first, until he told me it was you who'd been back o' that rifle.' Gilpin shook his head. 'My, but you're a dark one, Harry. You don't even own a horse, an' the way you kept that rifle hidden away is another thing that surprises me.'

Scratching his chin, Digweed said, 'That's something that bothers me about taking this job, Sheriff. I've never packed a handgun and I don't fancy starting now.'

'Then don't, Harry. A man carries a sidearm he's liable to get challenged an' shot at, but we're allus gettin' drifters through this way, like last Sunday, so you'll need t'be prepared. Carry your rifle around at all times, is my advice.'

'If I must, but it'll take some getting used to.'

'An' get it firmly fixed in your head that you may need t'make arrests. Don't shirk it.'

'That'll take some getting used to as well.'

'The first time'll be the hardest, but after that it gets easier. Remember there are trigger-happy drifters as well as a few local jaspers'll try t'take advantage of you. Wearin' that badge represents authority, but it ain't no picnic.'

Digweed sighed heavily. 'Maybe this is a mistake,' he said.

'After what you did yesterday, all you need t'do is focus on the job that somebody has t'do. Right now it's you. Won't be for long. I'll be back in harness in a day or two.'

Digweed nodded acquiescence, even though he knew it would be weeks rather than days. 'So what next?'

'Go show yourself around town an' let folks know you're no easy touch. The gossips will soon have it all over town it was you who killed four o' them outlaws yesterday. That'll make 'em sit up an' take notice. Just don't be modest about it, is all.'

It came to Harry Digweed quite suddenly that he had gone from being a murder suspect to a deputy sheriff overnight. Pride swelled within him. He'd been a nobody in Buzzards Creek ever since his arrival seven years ago, but now ...

He went out into the street with his head held high.

There was an outside stairway for access to or exit from the upper floor of the Eldorado Saloon, leading also to a balcony that ran the whole length of the rear aspect. The girls often used this east facing balcony to take the air after they had eaten breakfast. Their bedroom windows faced east, with the early morning sun casting light through the drapes. Rex Neeson's room was the last along the corridor. On this particular morning one of the rooms was vacant, that of the girl who had shared Neeson's bed that night. She was the newest arrival and had strict instructions not to share her favours with the clientele, but to keep herself only for him. He had not yet tired of her, although she knew he would when a fresh, interesting face came along.

'What time is it, Estelle?'

'According to my stomach it's time for coffee, then breakfast.'

'Go get it then, girlie.'

She reached for her robe and left to go to her own room to wash and dress.

Neeson yawned, stretched, and climbed out of the comfortable bed, scratching his thinning ginger head, moved to the window and flung back the drapes. The sight that met his eyes brought a startled exclamation from his lips.

'What the hell!'

His gaze was riveted on a length of rope hanging from the roof of the balcony. At its lower end it had been fashioned into a noose.

THIRTEEN

As the first waves of shock began to subside, the questions started to prowl around Rex Neeson's head.

Who had hung the noose there?

How long had it been dangling from that beam?

How many folks had already seen it?

That question prompted him to dress quickly and hurry out to remove the accusation that somebody was aiming his way.

He had not thought to bring a knife with him and he struggled to untie the knot around the cross-beam of the balcony roof. He eventually managed it, but not before two of the girls had looked out of their windows to see who was out there. He coiled the rope around his arm and glared at the girls, who quickly drew back. On his way back along the inside landing he entered both of their rooms and asked if they knew anything about it. Both girls offered him denials and their faces presented expressions of innocence.

Had they actually seen the noose?

He wasn't sure and, not wanting to put ideas into their heads, he did not ask them. He hurried back to his own room.

He sat on the edge of his bed and pondered who might suspect him of having strangled Jennie Clark, other than that damned Sheriff Gilpin?

Gilpin was, according to all reports, nursing bullet wounds in one of his legs and using crutches to hobble around his domestic quarters, so it was highly unlikely that he had been out there. He might, however, have engaged someone else to do it, just to see what the response would be?

Well he would soon find out. Neeson decided he would take the rope down to the Sheriff's Office and toss it onto his desk.

Then another thought struck him. What if Gilpin knew nothing about it?

In that event taking the rope to him and giving him a right rollicking would only offer the sheriff added reason to suspect him of killing Jennie Clark. No. It would be better to call in on Gilpin and offer his condolences. See if he made any mention of the girl's murder. Neeson didn't think the sheriff would be able to resist the chance of making capital out of the situation if he knew about that noose hung outside his bedroom.

But if it had not been put there at Gilpin's instigation, who else suspected him of strangling Jennie Clark?

He wracked his brain in vain. Not a single name came to mind. Could it be one of his own girls, resentful of the way she had been treated, who suspected him of the killing? Or one of Moe Langley's women, angered by the Clark girl's brutal murder?

Had Jennie told someone she was coming to see him after midnight on Saturday? And if so, who?

Hell and damnation!

No matter what he did or did not do would only make his position worse. He could figure out no way in which he would be any the wiser.

After the noontime meal out at the ranch Horace Idle grew steadily restless. In spite of what he had said to Walt Martin about teaching him the rudiments of his job, Idle felt totally out of place away from a town.

He reminded himself he had never had any interest in ranching and, as the afternoon wore on, he saddled his horse and climbed aboard.

'Where are you going, Uncle Horace?' young Zeke asked him as he hurried forward, his curiosity aroused.

'Tell your Ma I've gone into town, will you, Zeke?'

'Sure. Will you be back for supper?'

'I reckon not. See you in the morning, Zeke.'

Activity in The Four Aces was down to a minimum at four-thirty in the afternoon and Idle concentrated on enjoying the whiskey on offer. He could not get himself into a poker game and his thoughts began to dwell on what Laura Parker would be able to offer him, apart from her body, once she had swept away all the opposition to her acquisitive plans. The ranch, or even an interest in it, was not even an option, nor of any interest to him. Ten per cent of the timber yard might be. He guessed that the profits from the sale of timber would be much higher than those from the livery stables. The town appeared to be still growing and timber structures needed repairs from time to time. Then there were the rents from properties let out to Bob Reid and a few others. But either of those options seemed like small reward for the long trip he had made with Laura Parker and her son. He deserved more than that, he decided.

The store run by Ben Casey would be more to his liking. He might even allow the little feller to run it for him, so long as the profits ended up in Idle's pockets. After all, the ranch and the rents, the percentages from the timber yard and the livery ought to be enough for the woman and her son. They surely wouldn't begrudge him the store after all he had done for them – and may yet have to do – if they were to get what they wanted.

He decided to go and pay Casey a visit.

The liquor had warmed his belly but he was still in fairly good control of his senses when he walked into the store. Casey was serving a customer and Idle had enough perception to see it would be unwise to interrupt. Once the customer had left the store, Idle approached the counter. He noticed the patch of missing hair on the storekeeper's head that Doc

Rickman had cut away when he dressed the abrasion caused by Idle's gun.

'I'm just closing up, so whatever it is you want, come back tomorrow,' Casey told him brusquely.

The effrontery of the little man! Had he learned nothing from their previous encounter?

'Now don't you get stroppy with me, Casey, or I'll have to teach you another lesson. You opened that account for Mrs Parker at the bank yet?'

'No, I ain't and I've no intention of doing any such thing, so get out of here. Now!'

Fury exploded in Horace Idle and his right hand was instantly filled with his Smith and Wesson revolver, but as he reached across the mahogany counter to grab Casey's shirt front he got a shock he would never have expected. Ben Casey stepped back a pace and a gun was clutched in both hands, pointing straight at Idle's head.

'You make one more move, Idle, and I'll blow your head off.'

As he slowly recovered from this unexpected turn of events, a smile stretched Idle's mouth, revealing even, well-cared-for teeth.

There was irony in his voice as he spoke. 'Is that thing loaded, Casey?'

'You'd better believe it.'

'Then why don't you put it down before you do something you might regret?'

'I'll see you dead before you pistol-whip me again.'

With his gun aimed at Casey's chest, Idle asked, 'Do I have to kill you, or are you gonna see sense?'

'Stick your gun back in its holster and get out of here.'

The little man had more guts than Idle had expected.

'You think you could pull that trigger before I kill you?' he challenged in a manner designed to put doubt in Casey's mind.

'There's one sure way to find out,' Casey said evenly, knowing Idle would have to lift the gun now hanging by his side before he could use it, although even with that comforting thought his heart was pounding with fear.

Idle sighed with excessive exaggeration. He holstered his gun and said, 'And to think I only came in to talk.'

He turned as if to leave the store, expecting Casey to lower his own firearm, then after taking just three steps towards the door he swivelled quickly, drew and fired. But even as he turned, Ben Casey squeezed the trigger.

FOURTEEN

John Henry 'Doc' Holliday was visiting with the wounded sheriff, reminiscing about their days together in Dodge City, when their conversation was suddenly interrupted by the sound of gunfire. They looked at each other with questioning eyes.

'What in hell's goin' on now?' Gilpin snapped, hauling himself out of his chair and slipping the crutches under his armpits.

'Could be your deputy has found trouble,' Holliday surmised as he led the way to the street.

On the stoop he halted and looked first right and then left, with Gilpin clumping up behind him and doing likewise.

There were a few men on the street and their eyes were drawn towards Ben Casey's store. Others appeared out of doorways, curious to know what all the gunplay was about. Then they all saw Horace Idle stagger out of the store, left hand clutching his chest. He hurried down the street to the hitchrail outside The Four Aces saloon and hauled himself up to fork his horse, then turned the animal and kicked him into a fast lope, swaying in the saddle as he headed in the direction of the late Roger Talbot's ranch.

Harry Digweed came running down the street, rifle clutched in his hands, to watch the rapidly departing rider.

'Looks like Ben Casey stood up to the hard man,' the sheriff said as he clumped down off the stoop and headed for the store, with 'Doc' Holliday alongside him.

Digweed passed them at a run and followed men into the store to investigate what had happened. They found Ben Casey's wife bending over her husband. She looked up as they crowded round her behind the counter.

'Get the doctor!' she screamed at them. 'He's been shot!'

'I'll go,' one of the citizens volunteered.

Digweed laid his rifle on the counter. 'Let's get him into the parlour. Give me a hand.'

By the time the sheriff and Holliday joined them Ben Casey was lying on the couch, his eyes closed. There was no movement of his chest to indicate he was still breathing. Digweed laid an ear close to his heart.

'I can't hear anything,' he said solemnly, watching the dark stain spread on Casey's shirt.

'Oh, no! Oh, no!' his wife cried out, deeply distressed.

Digweed looked at the sheriff and shook his head briefly. Gilpin beckoned him with a flick of his own head and moved away. Digweed followed.

'It was Horace Idle. We'd best go after him. I reckon he was headed for the ranch.'

'But you can't ride with that foot, Sheriff!' Digweed exclaimed, glancing down at Gilpin's bandaged appendage.

'You wanna chase him on your lonesome?'

The sheriff knew he wouldn't and Digweed's face showed it.

'Get down to the livery. Saddle my horse an' bring him to me. Get a horse for yourself from George Taggart an' tell him why you want it. He'll probably not even make a charge once he knows what's happened. I'll cut the toe out o' my boot an' be ready by the time you come.' He turned to Holliday. 'John, I'll need a hand.'

The three men went out to the street, leaving the immediate fate of Ben Casey and his wife to the tender care of Doc Rickman. The medic was hurrying towards the store as the sheriff used his crutches with urgency for the first time.

'We think he's dead, Doc, but we ain't sure,' Gilpin told him.

There was no reply.

'You'll need to cut the top off that boot as well if you don't want to set that foot bleeding again, Jeff,' Holliday told him. 'You'll never get it on without doing more damage otherwise.'

Gilpin had already cut the upper leather back three inches from the toe. 'I guess you're right.' He sliced the calf off just above the ankle.

Taking considerable patience, Gilpin got the cut-down boot on with surprising ease. He smiled at Holliday. 'Looks a mess but at least I'll be able t'ride.'

Not without a lot of pain, you won't, Holliday decided, but he elected not to voice the thought. Instead he said, 'I'll go get my horse and ride along with you.'

'Thanks, John, only you'll have t'follow our dust. I think I hear Harry with our horses. Don't want t'give that varmint any more start than he's already gotten.'

He limped to unlock the chain that secured his rifle and two shotguns to the wall. He looked at Holliday. 'Want one?'

The card playing former dentist shook his head. 'Don't reckon you'll need one, either, with that ex-cavalry man siding you.'

But the sheriff ignored him and fisted the rifle, then secured the shotguns again before hobbling outside.

While Gilpin climbed cautiously into his saddle, Holliday hurried to the livery, just as one of the men who had gone into the store came along.

'Ben Casey's dead, Sheriff. Figured you'd want to know.'

'Thanks. Knowin' that makes what we have t'do a whole lot easier.'

Gilpin soon found shafts of pain stabbing through his wounded foot and up into his leg as he rode alongside Harry Digweed. He gritted his teeth and suffered, mindful of Walt Martin's warning about Horace Idle.

The newly appointed deputy, in spite of long years away from the saddle, had not forgotten how to ride. With his rifle in the scabbard, Digweed was mentally transported back to his days in the cavalry, rounding up renegade Indians who had rebelled against being herded into reservations set up for what had supposed to be for their benefit. A desire to avenge the killing of Ben Casey was uppermost in his mind. The thrill of the chase, with the county sheriff in support, lifted him. Get Idle and the threats to his boss, Chetwyn Handley, and others in Buzzards Creek would disappear. Without her protector Laura Parker would be toothless.

As they neared the ranch the sheriff called a halt in a motte of trees to discuss tactics.

'We don't know what's happenin' up there, Harry. No sense in makin' ourselves sittin' ducks for that trigger-happy galoot.'

'You think he'll be expecting us, Sheriff?'

'He will. My guess is he's run t' that woman t'get his wound dressed, but what he plans after that is anybody's guess.'

'How bad is he hurt?'

'He'll live, I reckon. He almost ran down the street t'get t'his horse after the shootin'. Just a flesh wound, maybe.'

'You think the woman will help him?'

'You reckon she has any option?'

'I guess not. But what about Walt Martin and his men? What will they do?'

'They'll be on our side, you can bet on it, but Walt

hates guns an' I doubt if he's gotten one in the house. He could become a hostage once Idle knows we're here.'

'So what do we do?'

'Wait. John Henry'll be here soon an' he might have some suggestions. My guess is that Idle will make a run for it once the woman can make him see sense. She ain't gonna be best pleased with what he's done, but she's gotten enough savvy t'know he'll be a wanted man. We don't want t'try an' take him from the ranch. He's gotten all the aces as long as he's there. Best t'let him run and then get him.'

'You don't think she'll go with him?'

'An' leave the boy? No way. My guess is that the property she's after is more important t'her than Horace Idle.'

They both turned at the sound of hoofbeats. 'Doc' Holliday was about to join them.

FIFTEEN

They were in the middle of supper when Horace Idle burst into the house. He ignored Walt Martin and the boy and spoke directly to the woman.

She jumped up from her chair at the table as she saw his blood-stained shirt.

'I've been shot, Laura,' he told her needlessly. 'I need your help.'

Martin pushed back his chair and said, 'I'll get you some bandages, Mrs Parker.'

When Ezekiel also stood up Martin said, 'You stay there and finish your supper, Zeke. There's nothing you can do. I'll help your mother attend to Mr Idle.'

He led the way out of the dining-room. 'Take him to his room, Mrs Parker. I'll be with you in a minute.'

In Idle's bedroom Laura Parker asked him what had happened.

'I went into the store to see if that little runt had done as we told him. He said he hadn't, had no intention of opening an account for the store takings in your name, then pulled a gun on me. He took me by surprise, I can tell you. Never would've thought he had it in him. Then he shot me as I was leaving.'

'Let me see.'

He removed his bloodied hand away from the wound and she began to unbutton his shirt. She saw the small hole where the bullet had entered the upper part of his chest, close to the left armpit. He had been hit at an angle and the bullet had exited behind, tearing an ugly gash below his arm. She knew it was not life threatening.

'That is going to be sore for a week or two,' she told him. Then a thought struck her. 'If he shot you as you were leaving you must have been walking backwards.'

He looked into her pale green eyes and found no words to reply.

'Let's have the truth, Horace.'

'I was turning around when he shot me.'

'And you fired back.' She made it a statement, as if there was no questioning what she surmised.

'Reckon I killed him, Laura. Hit him plumb centre.'

When Walt Martin came near to the door he heard her furious voice admonishing Idle. 'You fool! You blundering idiot! You'll have that sheriff after you now, you dumb-cluck. I told you not to start any trouble!'

'The sheriff is laid up with a wounded foot. He couldn't even straddle a horse.'

Martin decided it was a good time to interrupt. 'I've brought hot water from the stove, bandages, and some scissors, Mrs Parker. Anything more I can do to help?'

He looked at the blood-stained underwear. 'My, but that looks ugly, Mr Idle. How did it happen?'

The woman told him as she cut away Idle's blood-stained underwear around the shoulder and underneath the arm.

'Oh, dear,' Martin said solemnly. 'That means the sheriff will be coming out here.'

Idle winced as the woman began to clean up the wound, then favoured Martin with his most engaging smile. 'I doubt it, Martin. You seem to have forgotten he's laid low with a shot-up foot.'

If Idle had indeed killed Ben Casey, then not even a wounded foot would stop Gilpin doing something about it. He would organize a posse or something, ignore his own pain, and set out to capture Casey's killer. Martin was fully aware that Sheriff Jeff Gilpin was far tougher than most men. A killing in town, particularly one of Buzzards Creek's own citizens, would be an affront to his pride, and the sheriff was a very proud man when it came to his authority as its peace officer.

Martin knew it would serve no purpose to inform his unwelcome guest of these facts and remained silent. Ben Casey was a harmless, middle-aged man who would never hurt anyone and if he had been shot, then it was up to him, Walt Martin, to do whatever he could to assist in bringing the killer to justice. He just did not know how to go about it.

Laura Parker looked up. 'Go back and finish your supper, Mr Martin. Keep Ezekiel company. I don't want him coming in here.'

'You sure you can manage?'

'If I need you I'll give you a call.'

'As you wish.'

As soon as he had gone, fortunately closing the door behind him, the woman lowered her voice and hissed urgently, 'Just as soon as I've dressed this wound you get on your horse and run. I don't want this house riddled with bullets when a posse surrounds the place. You've done all you can for us. In fact you've probably ruined any hopes we ever had of pulling this thing off.'

'You mean I get nothing, after all the weeks I've put into this thing?'

'Didn't I just tell you? None of us will get anything now and it's all your stupid fault. You're so impetuous. I could kill you! I should've had more sense than to put my trust in a man who revels in violence and hurting people.'

'Aw, come on, Laura. I've been good for you. You can't deny that.'

'I expect far more of a man than being virile in bed!' she snapped back angrily.

When she had finished fixing a difficult job of dressing his wound he instructed her to get him some supper.

'You've no time for that! You're getting out of here now!'

'Oh, no, I'm not. I'm hungry.'

She raised her arms and clenched her fists in frustration. 'Don't you understand? There'll be a posse here any minute and if they catch you, you'll hang.

You've got to get away.'

'I'll go take a look, while you get that damned cook to serve me some supper . . . in the diner.'

Seeing there was no way of making him see reason she was obliged to play along. She went out of the room while he struggled into a clean shirt, then headed for the front door of the house to look around for any sign of men on his trail. There was no indication of pursuit.

The woman was right, of course. Sooner or later there would be a posse coming after him, but he figured he had an hour at least before they showed up. Time enough for him to eat and get that cook to fix him up with trail grub for his flight.

He hated to admit it, but he had messed things up for Laura and young Zeke, but then who would have thought that little runt in the store would have got himself a loaded gun and shot him? There was no way he could have anticipated that. Now there was nothing for it but to return to California. He would ride out in an hour, as daylight faded. He had gambled and lost with Laura Parker, but at least he'd had some good sessions with her when the boy had been out of the way. There were plenty more women in San Francisco. He would just have to forget about becoming a store owner and find some other woman with money who was looking for a man to protect her.

'You decided what you're going to do, Jeff?'

'Depends what Idle does, John. My guess is that once that woman has dressed his wound she'll persuade him to make a run for it. I reckon that would be our best time t'take him.'

'You could be right, only he might wait until dark before he makes his getaway. Be hard to follow then.'

'You got a better idea?'

'No, but I can see a few problems.'

'Such as?'

'That foot of yours for a start. I can tell it's giving you some pain. You need laudanum to help you. You need food and coffee in your belly. Have you thought about that?'

Gilpin had but he was not about to admit it. 'Didn't want t'get out here an' find he'd already gone. If'n I'd hung around to fix us up with grub we'd still be back there on the trail.'

'Then let's hope we get him as soon as he comes out, Jeff.'

'That's what I'm plannin' on, once he gets far enough away from the house.'

Harry Digweed decided he wanted his pennyworth in the discussion. 'In that case, Sheriff, we'd best split up. No telling which way he'll head: whether he'll come out through the back door or the front.'

'We keep an eye on his horse, Harry, then we'll know.'

'But he might take one of Walt's horses instead of his own.'

'You mean because he'll figure we're watchin' his?'

'Exactly. This ain't the first manhunt I've been on, Sheriff.'

'Never figured it was, Harry.'

The red blaze above the distant mountain peaks was already dying rapidly as silence settled on the trio. Eventually 'Doc' Holliday broke it.

'I think your deputy has a point, Jeff. I think we should separate.'

But before the sheriff could reply they heard the drumming of horses' hooves coming towards them. Within a minute Gilpin recognized the leading rider.

'It's George Taggart . . . an' Chet Handley . . . an' more men from town. What in hell. . . ?'

Harry Digweed ran forward, waving his arms to draw their attention. Taggart saw him and led the group into the trees. He made straight for the sheriff as soon as he dismounted, pulling something from a pocket.

'Doc Rickman sent you some laudanum, Sheriff. He figured you'd be badly in need of it. Instructed me to tell you you're a damn fool to go out riding with a wound like that.'

'Doc' Holliday grinned. 'He always was a reckless cuss.'

'Hi, there, Mr Holliday. Some of us decided you three might need a little help.'

'Indeed we do. We expect that killer down there to make a run for it any minute now. Be dark in next to no time. He must know he's trapped if he stays in that ranch house.'

'We'd best spread out and circle it then, don't you reckon?'

The sheriff conceded Taggart was probably right. He started counting. They now numbered twelve, enough to surround the house completely, but what were the ranch hands doing? Did they know that Idle was holed up in the house or had they been too busy eating supper to notice his arrival less than an hour ago?

'Any o' you men fancy makin' your way down t'the bunkhouse to find out what the hands are doin'?'

Digweed volunteered. 'Reckon I'm the best man for that job, Sheriff, what with my army training.'

'Bit of a dark horse, ain't you, Harry,' one of the men commented. 'You want I should come with you?'

Gilpin objected. 'Only needs one. I guess you're elected, Deputy. The rest of you spread out an' circle the house, but don't get too close 'til it gets dark. Idle has killed one man already today an' if he sees you he'll shoot. He knows he's got nothin' t'lose, so go carefully.'

He directed each man to where he wanted them to take up positions, except for 'Doc' Holliday.

'You'd best stay with me, John, seein' as you've no rifle. That gun o' yours ain't much use at this distance.'

SIXTEEN

Oblivious to the drama being enacted in the house, the ranch hands had settled down to telling tall tales of past experiences. Their eyes focused on the doorway at the sound of soft footfalls, then the opening was briefly darkened as Harry Digweed quickly entered and gazed around him.

He offered them a smile. 'Howdy, fellers. I'm Harry Digweed, as some of you already know. What you don't know is that I'm now Sheriff Gilpin's deputy.'

'You want we should congratulate you, Harry?'

'No. I want your help.'

'With what?'

He knew they were blissfully ignorant of what was going on in the house, so he told them about the shooting of Ben Casey.

'That bald-headed galoot shot ole Ben?'

'And killed him. We believe Idle is holed up in the house and we also think he'll be making a run for it any time now, so how many of you have gotten guns?'

'Boss don't believe in gunplay,' Digweed was told.

121

'That mean you're gonna sit around and do nothing to help?'

'What can we do?' another man countered. 'I've gotten a gun in my pack but I sure ain't goin' to face up to no killer with it.'

'Then just sit tight, all of you, and that's an order. Your boss may well become a hostage if any of you do anything stupid to alert that Idle feller that I'm here.'

'You can count on us, Deputy.'

'Good. I don't think he knows I'm here yet.'

'You here on your lonesome?'

'No. There's a dozen of us. We've gotten the house surrounded.'

'What you aim t'do?'

'Watch his horse. It's made its own way to the barn. Wants a feed, I guess. Idle must've been in such an all-fired hurry to get his wound dressed he didn't waste time hitching it. I'm gonna see if I can get to the barn without being seen from the house.'

'No chance,' he was told. 'Leastways not while it's still light.'

'You stay away from that bunkhouse, Cookie. Pack me enough trail grub to last for three days and don't let me hear a squawk out of you or I'll put a bullet in your belly. You savvy?'

'Sure, Mr Idle, sure. I get the grub for you.'

Idle looked out of the window again and fancied he saw movement in the motte of trees three hundred yards from the house. If that posse had already arrived he would need something to change the odds that would be stacked against him. He would need a hostage to take along with him.

The woman or the boy?

Laura Parker had already made herself unpopular with some of the folks in town so maybe those men out there – assuming he had not imagined that movement – might not care too much if she took a bullet, as long as they shot or captured him. It would have to be the boy.

He had been sent to his room, so Idle sidled quietly along the corridor. He knocked on the closed door and entered. The fair-haired Ezekiel looked up from the book he was reading.

'Hello, Uncle Horace.'

'Put your coat on, Zeke. I want you to take a ride with me.'

'But it's nearly dark. Where are we going?'

Coaxing the boy would be better than forcing him. During that long ride from San Francisco Idle had completely won his confidence. Telling him as little as possible would add to the mystery of the ride.

'Not far. It's just that I need your help with something. You don't mind helping me, do you, Zeke?'

'Of course not.'

The boy got up and reached for his coat. Idle knew his mother was in consultation with Walt Martin and if they could sneak out without alerting them a nasty confrontation would be avoided.

Before they moved out into the corridor Idle whispered, 'Let's not tell your Ma, Zeke. She might object to me taking you out so late.'

Ezekiel smiled conspiratorially, his youthful curiosity aroused. 'Right,' he whispered back.

They went out through the kitchen, where the cook was just wrapping the grub Idle had ordered.

'You want this now, Mr Idle?'

Idle nodded and took the package silently. He opened the door and ushered the boy ahead of him. 'Head for the barn, Zeke.'

One window in the bunkhouse looked out towards the barn and Harry Digweed elected to watch from safety. After ten patient minutes he cursed softly. 'Hell and damnation! He's got the boy with him!'

He turned around and looked at the men. Dan Foster said, 'You mean he's takin' the kid hostage?'

The hands crowded round Digweed, trying to see what was happening. 'They're already in the barn,' Harry told them.

'What you gonna do now?' The question came again from Foster.

'I have to alert the others. They might hit the boy if it comes to a shoot-out.'

As he made for the door Dan Foster said, 'Hold it, Harry. Why don't you stay here an' see what happens while I go tell the others for you?'

The offer sounded good to Digweed but a tiny doubt troubled him. 'You'd have to go carefully. If Idle sees you he'll maybe guess what you're up to and he won't hesitate to shoot.'

Foster reached for his hat. 'Just tell me where they are.'

*

In the rapidly fading daylight George Taggart had moved closer to the ranch buildings, using the blind spot from the house created by the position of the bunkhouse. He wasn't sure what to expect but he knew the deputy was inside. He had kept his eyes on Digweed as the former soldier had bellied forward earlier, while the light was still good. He had seen him rise to his feet and hurry to the bunkhouse door once he was within easy striking distance. Now Taggart was lying full length, rifle pointing towards the house, waiting for something to happen. When he saw someone leave the bunkhouse and run towards him he raised his head, wondering if it was Harry Digweed or one of the ranch hands. As the man drew closer Taggart called softly.

'Over here!'

Dan Foster faltered in his run, his eyes searching the gloom.

'Get down, you fool!' Taggart warned. 'They'll see you!'

Foster crouched and headed to where the voice seemed to be coming from, stumbling down alongside Taggart moments later. He was panting as he dropped to the ground.

'What's happened?' Taggart asked impatiently.

'That big feller has taken the boy as a hostage. Harry Digweed sent me to tell you.'

'I never heard the boy cry out. Has Idle gagged him?'

'No. Harry reckoned Idle has conned the boy into goin' with him. The kid don't know what's goin' on. Where are the others?'

'Surrounding the house. You want to stay here while I go and warn them?'

'No, I don't have a gun. I'd best be messenger. Who's closest an' where is he?'

'Chet Handley is away to our left but maybe not as close as this. Go carefully with your arms held out so's he don't mistake you for that killer.'

Chet Handley had seen Dan Foster leave the bunkhouse and guessed he had stumbled on Taggart. As Foster ran in a crouch towards him he could see he was not carrying a gun. Once he had been given the news he sent Foster on his way to tell the others.

It was a mission that was not devoid of danger.

'Doc' Holliday called out, 'Hold it right there, mister, or I'll blow your head off.'

Foster spread his arms out wide. 'Don't shoot! I'm only the messenger.'

'Come forward.'

'It's Dan Foster,' the sheriff told Holliday. 'He's one of the hands. Come on in, Dan.'

By the time they had saddled Ezekiel Parker's pony, moved out of the barn and mounted, the gloom had thickened. Idle decided it was hardly likely that either Walt Martin or Laura Parker would be looking out of a window but, just in case he and the boy were still visible fron the house, he decided to head away

towards the town before turning in an arc to ride
west. He kept the boy riding alongside him in case
there were possemen circling the house, thinking
that if any of them considered taking a shot at him
they would think again in case they hit the youngster.
Once heading in the direction he wanted to go,
maybe with the posse strung out behind them, he
could let Zeke return to the ranch. In the dark, Idle
himself would be a difficult target to hit.

Harry Digweed cussed until he went red in the face.
Good shot though he was, he did not dare to risk
firing in the near darkness for fear of hitting the boy,
who was riding very close to Idle. Digweed's mount
was more than three hundred yards away, up in those
trees, and he could not follow the fugitive for long
on foot. His best plan would be to hurry back to the
sheriff and let him know which way Idle and the
youngster were riding.

Gilpin and Holliday were already mounted and
moving in his direction when Digweed got back to
them, breathing hard and finding words difficult to
get out.

'Idle's gotten . . . the boy with him. They're . . .
headed . . . towards town.'

'Town!' Gilpin spat in surprise.

'It's a ploy of some kind, Jeff,' Holliday said. 'He'll
double back, I would imagine.'

'Get mounted, Harry, an' go tell the others t'come
an' get their horses. Me an' John will get after them.'

'I've no idea if . . . he knows we're here, but . . . taking the boy . . . suggests to me he does. He'll kill him, Sheriff . . . if he has to.'

Gilpin's foot was giving him hell and he had not dared to take the laudanum Doc Rickman had sent out in case it made him drowsy, dimming his faculties. He was irritable.

'You think I don't know that? Get mounted and go tell the others.'

'No need . . . to bite my head off.'

SEVENTEEN

An awkward silence had developed between Walt Martin and Laura Parker. Both of them had talked as if they were treading on hot coals, every step a cautious one. There had been a degree of frankness, tinged with the fear of how what was said might be received, neither wanting to stress too much what would transpire as a result of the exchange of shots between Idle and Ben Casey.

'In spite of Mr Idle's confidence, Mrs Parker, Sheriff Gilpin will not ignore the shooting of Ben Casey. He will come here somehow, even if he has to get someone to drive him in a buggy.'

'I know that, Mr Martin.' She was still tense with anger. 'If only Horace had listened to me. I told him not to antagonize any of the people in town, but he's so impetuous.'

Martin said quietly, 'What has happened in town this afternoon won't have helped your claims, I'm afraid.'

Her eyes were sombre as they settled on him once again. 'And how about you, Mr Martin? Will what has happened change your attitude to me and Ezekiel?'

'I don't honestly know, Mrs Parker. I had a great respect for Ben Casey. He was a hard-working, respected citizen in Buzzards Creek. A lot of people liked him.'

'But you do believe that Ezekiel really is Roger Talbot's son, don't you?'

Martin still harboured a faint reluctance to accept the claim, even though the boy's facial features could well develop into something strongly resembling the dead tyrant. Funny how that title came to mind, when it was others who had described him so. To Walt Martin, Roger Talbot had been a good employer, leaving him to run the ranch unhampered by constant questioning of what he was doing or how forward planning was going. Martin had given Talbot reports three or four times a year, but a healthy return on the dead man's investment was all he ever cared about. The alliance suited them both, leaving Martin to enjoy what he was doing.

'You seem reluctant to answer me, Mr Martin.'

Exercising restraint, Martin answered, 'I think he could be, and I like the boy. If he were my son I would be very proud of him. You've raised him well, but that certificate is the only proof you can offer that Zeke is Talbot's son. I doubt if the townsfolk will be quite so ready to accept your claim.'

'I can understand that, but I give you my word, Ezekiel is Talbot's rightful heir to the property he left. To the best of my knowledge Roger was never married and he has no other children.'

'No brothers? Sisters? Cousins?'

'No. Like Ezekiel, Roger Talbot was born out of wedlock. That fact may well account for his ruthlessness. He had to fight for everything he got. There was no one to fight for him. It made him very determined to succeed.'

A silence developed while Martin assimilated this new information the woman had revealed about his former employer.

It was Laura Parker who spoke again first as she got out of her chair. 'I'd best go say goodnight to my son, if you'll excuse me.'

'Of course.'

A minute later he heard her calling outside the house. 'Where are you, Zeke? Time you were in bed. Come along now.'

Walt Martin went outside to join her. 'He wasn't in his room?'

'No. Whatever possessed him to go out so late? Maybe he's gone down to talk with the hands in the bunkhouse?'

'I wouldn't have thought so, but I'll go and check.'

As he approached the bunkhouse the men came filing outside.

'Have any of you seen the boy?'

They all began to speak at once and Talbot's fears were instantly realized. He hurried back to Laura Parker.

'He's gone out riding with Mr Idle.'

'In the dark?'

As they stared at each other she tried to resist the

fear that was dawning in her mind, but when Martin remained so silent she was compelled to accept the truth. 'He's gone on the run, hasn't he, and taken Ezekiel with him as a hostage?'

'I'm afraid it looks that way.'

'How far are we going, Uncle Horace?'

Idle was still not sure if he had been mistaken in what had seemed like human movement in those trees, but he did know there had been enough time for a posse to reach the ranch from town. It could well have been no more than two or three men up there watching the house, which would account for him and Zeke getting away without interference, although he was not prepared to dismiss the possibility that there was a larger number of men in search of retribution and that the house had been surrounded. In that event, having Zeke with him had probably saved him from a rifle bullet in the back.

The boy was puzzled by this half circular route they seemed to be taking and the man's preoccupation with his own thoughts. He tried again. 'Uncle Horace?'

'Yes, Zeke? What were you saying?'

'How far are we going?'

'I'm not sure yet.'

Keeping the boy with him would give him a bargaining factor if the posse ever caught up with them. But he had grown to like Zeke. He was different. Always so polite and respectful and Idle had not often encountered those qualities in the young. He liked it. It was good to have Zeke call him 'uncle', even though the youngster knew they were not really related. Once he had put distance between himself and the ranch he could let Zeke return to his mother.

'Let's put the horses into a lope, Zeke. Make better time.'

'Won't that be dangerous in the dark?'

'Not now we're on the trail. It's well defined.'

Three miles farther on he drew rein and the boy looked at him questioningly.

'Listen, Zeke, can you hear anything?'

The boy tilted his head. 'Horses? Getting closer?'

'That's right, Zeke. Let's ride!'

Idle pushed his mount into eating up the miles, with Ezekiel Parker, afraid of being left alone in strange, darkened country, doing his best to keep up. Fear began to take a grip on him. What was his Uncle Horace doing racing away from the ranch at this time of night, and with a wounded chest?

'Slow down!' the sheriff yelled. 'We don't want him t'hear us comin' up behind him.'

'Why not, Sheriff?' Chet Handley questioned.

'Because he'll move off the trail an' let us ride past.'

'Then take a different route, you mean?'

'That's what I mean. We could ride through the night an' be miles ahead o' him without knowin' it. Pull up, all o' you. Let's listen for hoofbeats.'

After a few moments Harry Digweed said, 'He's

racing that horse, Sheriff. Sound is getting faint fast.'

'You're right, Harry. We'll follow at a walk 'til we can be sure he's still on the trail. He might think he's safe until daybreak.'

'Uncle Horace! Slow down!'

Idle pulled on the reins. 'What's wrong, Zeke?'

'My pony is getting tired. Can't we go back now?'

Idle drew to a halt, the boy doing likewise. The man listened for following horses and heard nothing.

'Think you can find your way back to the ranch alone, Zeke?'

'Why? Aren't you going back?'

'Yes, Zeke, back to California. You see, boy, I killed a man this afternoon, when he shot me, and the sheriff's men will be coming after me. They think I murdered that man.'

'Did you?'

'No, Zeke, it was self-defence, only I'm a stranger in Buzzards Creek and they won't believe that. I have to get away. It's what your Ma wants me to do.'

'Did she say that?'

'Yes.' Idle could see disappointment settle on the boy. 'You go back, Zeke. I expect your mother will be getting worried about you by now. It's goodbye time for you and me. Off you go.'

Reluctant to obey, disillusion rising within him, Ezekiel now knew that 'Uncle Horace' had used him to get away and would have taken him as a hostage if the posse had caught up with them. This man had known they were being followed, and that was why they had ridden so fast after they'd heard hoofbeats behind them.

He turned his pony, afraid that he might not find his way back to the ranch, yet knowing he would never see 'Uncle Horace' again.

He did not even say goodbye.

EIGHTEEN

Almost out of her mind with worry, Laura Parker paced up and down outside the house, clenching and unclenching her fists, her eyes searching the darkness, ears listening for the sound of hoofbeats, her taut nerves shutting out the cold. Walt Martin was with her, huddled into his thick coat, yet shivering in the hour before dawn.

For the seventh time the woman turned to him and wailed, 'Why didn't we go with them? What are we doing here when Ezekiel is in this terrible danger?'

'I told you before, Mrs Parker. The sheriff wants us here in case Zeke comes back. He has enough men with him to deal with the situation. He needs us here to take care of Zeke when he gets back.'

'*If* he gets back, you mean! Horace is using Ezekiel to protect himself!'

'I know, but the boy trusts him and whatever we may think of Idle, it was my impression he likes the boy. I don't believe he means to harm him.'

She snapped back sharply, 'You don't know anything about Horace Idle! That storekeeper is not the first man he's killed. Why do you think I hired him to bring us here in the first place?'

'I've wondered about that. Why did you?'

'Because I knew he was afraid of no man and he would kill to protect me and Ezekiel if he had to. He can be the most charming man alive when it suits him, but he would kill a man as easily as you might swat a fly.'

That I can believe, Martin agreed silently.

'The sheriff and his posse will get him, Mrs Parker, but they will not do anything that would put Zeke in jeopardy.'

'You wouldn't be so sure about that if he was *your* son!' she retorted angrily. 'And you wouldn't be standing around here doing nothing!'

Riding alongside the sheriff, 'Doc' Holliday knew by the droop of his shoulders and the grimace which kept crossing his bearded face with greater frequency that Gilpin was in terrible pain. They were walking the horses to give them a breather and Holliday was moved to call a halt.

'What's gotten into you, John?' the sheriff queried.

'You need to take that laudanum, Jeff. Don't try telling me you're not in agony. It shows on your face.'

Harry Digweed, riding on the other side of the sheriff, had also noticed he was in considerable pain. 'He's right, Sheriff. What's more, you need to wrap something around that foot. With no protection from the cold that wound will be getting worse.'

Gilpin knew they were both right but he was reluctant to admit it. As the other members of the posse crowded round them he questioned grumpily, 'You gotten anythin' t'wrap around it?'

Frank Walmsley, the blacksmith, eventually surrendered the bandanna he habitually wore to wipe the sweat from his brow while he was working at the furnace, and this was tied carefully over the boot that no longer had a toe. Having come from around Walmsley's neck it had a little warmth in it.

'Thanks, Frank.'

'You're welcome, Sheriff.'

'Now take some of that laudanum,' Holliday instructed.

Nerves frayed to almost breaking point by the intense pain, Gilpin needed no further encouragement, but he did limit the amount he took for fear of losing all feeling. When they eventually caught up with the fugitive he wanted to be in full control of his faculties so that he could direct operations.

Holliday knew how his mind was working. 'There's enough of us here to deal with that man, Jeff, without you worrying about it. You've got a deputy alongside you who probably knows nigh on as much as you about tracking fugitives, him being an old army man.'

Gilpin glared at his old friend, unwilling to acknowledge the truth of what Holliday was saying.

'Let's move. We don't want that varmint gettin' too far ahead of us. Be dawn in an hour, then we can follow his trail.'

*

Horace Idle, suffering with pain and lack of sleep, had slowed his horse to a walk. His wound felt as if it was on fire and he knew he needed medical help, yet he had no idea where to find it until he had ridden another forty miles. He needed rest, he told himself. In spite of the cold he felt confident that two hours' sleep would do him a world of good; give him a sharpness of mind to cope with whatever that posse could throw at him. He was positive he still had a good lead on then, but if they should catch up, they would still have to find him. The moon shone on boulders and rock strata away to his left and they would offer him cover. He steered his mount off the trail and ground hitched him, then removed his saddle and blankets. He found a soft spread of earth behind a huge boulder and spread out his tarp.

Covering himself with his blanket, head resting in the hollow of his saddle, he silently cursed Ben Casey. Underestimating a man was not normally one of his weaknesses. He had misjudged badly with Casey.

Weariness eventually won the battle against the throbbing in his chest and sleep claimed him.

The first hint of dawn came just as Sid Gallard brought Ezekiel Parker within sight of the ranch house. The boy was wearied and so was his pony. He could not even summon the enthusiasm to hurry the animal forward to greet his mother's running figure heading his way.

'Zeke! Oh, Zeke! You're safe,' she blurted as he practically fell out of the saddle into his mother's embrace. 'I thought I'd lost you.'

Walt Martin went and stood beside Sid Gallard as he dismounted, both of them silenced by the touching scene being played out before them.

'Reckon she's glad to have him back,' Gallard eventually said with a tired smile. 'You gotten any coffee on the stove, Walt?'

'I'll soon fix you some, Sid. We'll hitch Zeke's pony and your horse before we go inside. You can tell me all about it while we wait for the java to heat up.'

'Nothing much to tell. We met the boy riding back here a couple of hours ago. Sheriff asked for a volunteer to make sure he got back safely. Guess I just got me elected.'

'Had Idle let him go or did the boy guess what was happening and make a break for it?'

'No. That murdering bastard let him go once he figured he'd outstripped us.' He pushed out a long, tired sigh. 'You know what they say, Walt; there's some good even in the worst of men.'

'I think Idle had become like a father to him. In fact Zeke always called him "Uncle".'

'They'd gotten bonded then, huh?'

'Yes, I do believe they had. I'm afraid Zeke will be badly disillusioned by what has happened these last twelve hours.'

'At least the boy is back with his mother. They say she's a hard woman, but I guess she's as soft as most women when it comes to their sons.'

*

His sign was easy to follow once the night had gone and the new day shed its light on the trail. Idle had made no attempt to conceal his progress and that fact alerted both the sheriff and his deputy to impending trouble.

'Doc' Holliday said, 'He'll be waiting up ahead to find out how many of us are on his trail, Jeff.'

'That's what I'm thinkin'. Trouble is, he'll proba-bly see us afore we see him. Eleven men an' their horses can't hide easily, but one man might.'

Gilpin called a halt and the men gathered around him. He explained his fears to them.

'If Idle is any good with a rifle he'll try an' pick us off one by one, so we have t'be careful. Me an' Harry'll go on ahead t'see if his sign peters out some place. You fellers hang back at least a quarter mile. If you hear any shots, come runnin', but spread out so's you don't make easy targets for Idle. Understood?'

Too tired to argue, they grunted and nodded acceptance.

Only a mile farther on the hoof prints of Idle's horse no longer led directly forward.

'He turned off here, Sheriff,' Digweed said. 'He could be hiding up in those rocks. We'd best take cover before he sees us.'

'If you're right, why ain't he opened fire already?'

'Could be he's fallen asleep. We don't know how badly he's wounded, but riding all night won't have helped him none. He must be as tuckered out as you, and he ain't had no laudanum to ease the pain Casey's bullet's been giving him.'

'Then let's separate. I'll go t'the left o' that big boulder up yonder, you go t'the right. If you get a bead on him, give him the chance t'surrender, but if he don't drop his gun, shoot good an' fast afore he shoots you.'

Horace Idle stirred in his sleep and pain shafted through him, bringing him back to consciousness. He unhinged stiffened, creaking knees, opened his eyes and discovered the sun was already rising to bring warmth to the new day.

He looked around him.

His horse was trying to find a few blades of grass close by, but he would need more than was available there to put new life into his belly.

Idle was thirsty and he reached for his water bottle to take a drink. Hunger had not yet stirred in him, but as recollection of what he was doing in this forlorn place came back to him he knew the danger was not over. If that posse had continued through the night they must be close by, or maybe they had already passed him.

He wondered if his sign petering out had been noticed? If that sheriff or his deputy were any good at reading sign they would surely have seen he had left the main trail.

He struggled painfully to his feet. The dressing Laura Parker had fixed for him was blood-stained and sticking to his torn flesh. It dragged as he moved.

He picked up his rifle from where he had lain it down and saw it was covered with frost. He wiped it with his handkerchief and moved to the edge of the huge boulder which had sheltered him from prying eyes.

'Drop it, Idle!'

His head swivelled in the direction of the sound and he saw Sheriff Gilpin clearly outlined above rocks away to his right. Idle wrapped his forefinger around the trigger and fired quickly, without taking aim, diving away to his right as he did so.

Gilpin's return shot missed him by inches, then the lawman ducked out of sight.

'You see him, Harry?' Gilpin called out.

'Yeah, I see him, Sheriff.'

But Digweed didn't. Prudence dictated that he should give the sheriff an affirmative reply to make Idle think he was completely surrounded, which would allow Digweed to move up higher and get a better look now that he had some idea where Idle's shot had come from. He scampered up the slippery slope as best he could, sliding back several times before he caught sight of Gilpin.

But he still could not see Horace Idle.

The thunder of horses' hooves reached his ears. Now they would get that murdering swine. Within minutes he would be surrounded.

NINETEEN

One to his right and another to his left, but how many more? Idle asked himself. Crouching, he moved with as much speed as wisdom would allow. No sense in putting his foot in a crevice and getting himself stuck. He needed to gain height, sensing that the other men would also move now that his shot had given away his position. Idle knew his life might well depend upon which of them could climb the highest in the shortest space of time. As he searched for fresh foot and hand holds the early morning sun temporarily blinded him. He turned his head to look the other way and caught a glimpse of the man he recognized as Gilpin's deputy. He lifted his rifle to take aim, but by the time he had gotten it to his shoulder the man had disappeared again behind a jagged upshoot of rock.

He knew it was the deputy who presented the biggest threat. With that wounded foot, the sheriff would not be able to do much climbing and had probably fought against pain to get as far as he had already. A grim smile stretched his lips. So long as he

144

kept out of sight of the sheriff it was one man against another and Idle felt confident he could win that battle.

Sounds behind him made him turn his head. Down below other men were spreading out, forsaking their saddles and taking cover, their eyes searching the sloping rocky terrain, but as yet they had not spotted him.

He did not hear George Taggart, alongside 'Doc' Holliday, ask, 'You see any of them?'

'Not a one. They're up there somewhere, playing cat and mouse with each other.'

'Plenty of places a man could hide up there.'

'You're right about that.' Holliday was telling himself he had been a fool to allow friendship to drag him into a situation that was totally foreign to him. Killing a man in a saloon was nothing new to him and gave him few qualms, but out here at the foot of a mountain, he felt like a trout out of water. Gilpin had a deputy, so what the hell was Holliday doing alongside a man he had met only once before, sliding about on rock? 'Wonder if any of those shots we heard found their target?' he asked Taggart, resigned to seeing the hunt through to the end.

'We're sitting ducks here, Mr Holliday. Let's get in closer.'

Idle knew he could pick off several of those men heading his way, but even as he lifted the rifle to his shoulder he thought better of it. His shot sound would give away his new position and draw the others nearer. Time to reassess his chances.

They now knew roughly where he was and, unless he killed every last one of then, he had no chance of getting away. The next thing he heard only confirmed that conclusion.

'Sheriff!' someone yelled. 'We've found his horse. We've gotten him boxed in.'

There was no answer from the sheriff but Gilpin, fighting his pain, felt a warm glow flooding through him. Minus his horse, Idle had no means of getting away. It was now just a question of time.

Where had Harry gotten to? Had his deputy improved his position? That was the trouble with a manhunt that developed this way; the mouse often had more advantages than the cat and Horace Idle was playing the game well.

The fugitive was not too disturbed by the know-ledge that his horse had been discovered. There were plenty of horses spread around below him and, once he had disposed of the men, he could take his pick, saddle and all. His gunbelt was full of shells and so far he had only used one from the breech of his rifle. There were five in his Smith and Wesson revolver for close shots. So long as he didn't waste any he still had a slim chance of disposing of Sheriff Gilpin and the whole of his posse.

Harry Digweed, higher up the mountainside now, got a brief glimps of Idle as he, too, climbed farther up, but too fleeting to take aim and call out to him to surrender. Below him, Digweed could see three of the townsfolk edging upwards, but under their broad-brimmed hats, with little else showing, he failed to recognize any of them. He longed to call out a warning, knowing that if he could see them, then it was highly likely that Horace Idle could too, but Harry was reluctant to betray the advantage of a higher spot that matched Idle's own.

Sheriff Gilpin, settling himself as comfortably as he could, eyes turned to scan upwards and to his left, fretted silently, not knowing what was happening either above or below him, so well had he shielded himself against the possibility of the fugitive being able to get a bead on him. He felt frustrated and useless by his inability to take a more active part in the hunt and the feeling angered him. The thought that Digweed could end up dead, just because he had recruited him as a deputy, added to his misery. Never in all his years as a lawman had he been so handicapped to perform his duties as a badge toter.

He could hear the scuffing of boots on rock as members of his posse scrabbled around, trying to see either him, Harry Digweed, or Horace Idle. The killer must surely be able to see at least some of them. When would he start shooting? He must know that his only chance of flight was to kill every last one of them. Even as the thought came to him, so did the sound of three shots with no more than a half second in between them. The shots were followed by cries of anguish and falling bodies. The carnage had begun.

Harry Digweed, alerted to Idle's position by the shot sound, stood up and got a clear view of the killer.

'Drop the rifle, Idle, or you're a dead man!' Harry called loudly.

It needed only the second in which Idle turned to face him, rifle nestling in the hollow of his shoulder, to convince him that the killer was not going to comply.

They both squeezed their triggers simultaneously.

TWENTY

As the echoes died away, a silence so pronounced settled on the mountainside that it turned the men into statues for almost a minute, while each one, including Sheriff Gilpin, asked himself what the shots would reveal. One by one they stood up cautiously, half expecting nore shooting, but the silence remained, until Chet Handley saw Horace Idle lying grotesquely spreadeagled over a boulder, his head tilted backwards, right arm outstretched, the left lying across his body.

'Looks like Harry got him, Sheriff!' Handley yelled. 'He ain't moving.'

'Go check, Chet,' Gilpin called back, 'but keep your gun on him 'til you're sure he's dead.'

A minute later Handley responded. 'He's as dead as a dodo. Come on up.'

Following the sound of his voice, the others slowly advanced and gathered around the dead man, apart from the three Horace Idle had shot. 'Doc' Holliday and Frank Walmsley went in different directions. Holliday finally located the sheriff and asked if he needed any help climbing down to the flat ground again.

'Guess I might need a hand, John. Allus harder goin' down than climbin' up. Harder still with this damned foot.' He turned his head and yelled to the others. 'Bring that killer's body down, will you?'

'Will do, Sheriff,' two of them answered in unison.

Meantime Frank Walmsley was trying to locate Harry Digweed, who had disappeared from sight and was making no audible sound.

When he eventually came upon him Harry was lying against a jagged rock, eyes closed, his knees buckled awkwardly, his rifle settled in a small crevice where he had dropped it. Walmsley noticed the dark stain on Digweed's vest and blood was trickling from his mouth. At the sound of his footfalls Harry opened his eyes.

'You hurt bad, Harry?' Walmsley asked him, feeling stupid. It was obvious even to his untrained eyes that Digweed's wound was serious.

'I'm done for . . . Frank.'

'You hang in there, Harry. We'll soon get you down from here.' Walmsley called out urgently. 'Get up here, some of you. Harry's hurt bad. Come on!'

He knelt down beside the deputy as Digweed coughed and more blood shot from his mouth in a small torrent.

His eyes closed again and then opened seconds later. 'Tell . . . the sheriff. . . .'

'What, Harry? What do you want me to tell him?'

'Jennie . . . Clark. Tell him . . . it was . . . me.'

'You!' Walmsley's astonishment was betrayed in the single word. 'You don't mean . . . You can't mean it was you who strangled her?'

Their eyes locked briefly. 'Yes . . . it was. . . .'

He coughed again and yet more blood burst out between his lips.

As Frank Walmsley continued to stare at him in disbelief, Harry Digweed's eyelids slowly shuttered and his head rolled a little more to the right. His body quivered just once and then was still.

Twenty minutes later they were all assembled again on the edge of the trail that led back to Buzzards Creek. Harry Digweed and Horace Idle were not the only two dead amongst them. Idle had killed one man and wounded two others, but fortunately his aim had not been as steady with his two second shots, taken hurriedly. The men were bleeding and in pain, but their wounds were not life threatening once a tourniquet had been applied to the leg of one and a chest wound plugged on the other. As they all moved off, Frank Walmsley rode up alongside the sheriff and 'Doc' Holliday.

'Sheriff . . .' Walmsley wasn't sure how to impart the news he had for him.

'Yes, Frank. what is it?'

'Something Harry asked me to tell you.'

'I think I can guess, Frank, but you'd best spell it out.'

Walmsley's eyes stared back, mystified. 'You can guess?'

Gilpin was in pain, tired and irritable. 'Aw, come on, Frank, quit stallin'! Harry told you it was him as strangled that girl, didn't he?'

'Yes, but . . . how did you know?'

Gilpin let out a long, heavy sigh which indicated his own sadness. 'They'd been havin' somethin' goin', the two o' them. He thought it was all gonna end because of. . . .' Gilpin's voice trailed away as he considered how much to keep to himself. Then he went on, 'He admitted he'd been jealous. Even tried to put me off by tellin' me he'd put the rope around the killer's neck himself if'n he'd known who it was. Almost had me fooled into believin' him, but I still figured he was the one with most motive. Nothin' like the green-eyed monster for changin' a man.

'In my mind he was the only one I could really suspect, only I'd never've been able t'take him into court without a confession. I guess Harry couldn't kick in without gettin' it off his chest.'

'So what are you going to do about it? Let folks think the man who killed Ben Casey's murderer was a killer himself?'

'I guess that's a problem I'm stuck with, Frank. The fact that he killed Idle don't excuse him for stranglin' the girl. If I say nothin' I'll be accused o' fallin' down on the job again. Two women strangled an' no arrests made. That could lose me my job.'

John Henry Holliday said quietly. 'That's a choice I'd hate to have to make, Jeff.'

While the others continued into town, Holliday and

Gilpin stopped off at the ranch to inform Laura Parker that Horace Idle was dead. Both she and Ezekiel had gone to bed exhausted but sleep had eluded her. When she heard voices she could not contain her curiosity, so she dressed quickly and went to see who had called. She took the news of Horace Idle's death badly, knowing there was no dividend for her in learning about what had happened that morning, miles up along the trail they had covered together in the opposite direction less than a week earlier.

'You intend to stay here now, Mrs Parker, now that Idle is dead?' Gilpin questioned, the urge to know more strong than even he would have considered reasonable.

She cogitated over her response for a long half minute. 'This ranch and that store in town rightfully belong to my son, Sheriff, and I intend to do what I can to see that he inherits them.'

Gilpin looked at Walt Martin. 'I could use some breakfast, Walt, then maybe you'd tell me how you feel about that?'

'Surely, Sheriff. I'll get cookie to fix it.'

Laura Parker said, 'If you'll excuse me, Sheriff, I have nothing more to say.'

'I'll be seeing you again, ma'am, I've no doubt, but for now, you get back to your rest. You've had a bad night, I reckon.'

'Indeed I did.'

She turned and left the room, while Martin invited his two visitors to take the weight off their feet. 'You want me to take a look at that foot of yours, Sheriff?'

'No, thanks, Walt. I've put up with it all night, I reckon it can wait 'til Doc Rickman can fix me a new dressing. I'll take the rest o' this laudanum. It might just take the edge off the soreness.'

He knew that 'soreness' was a huge understatement, but he was determined not to let them see the pain was driving him crazy.

Frank Walmsley was considerably disturbed about the problem facing Sheriff Gilpin. He did not want the townsfolk to think that Harry Digweed had been a murderer. In spite of his hot temper, Harry had been a very popular man. And yet it did not seem right that folks should blame Gilpin for not resolving the issue of Jennie Clark's killing when both of them now knew the truth. By the time he had wolfed down a late breakfast he made up his mind that, in spite of what he owed to the dead man, the living were more important.

After the sheriff returned to town the mayor came to see him, just as Doc Rickman was cleaning up his wounded foot.

'Fate decrees some funny twists and turns, eh, Jeff?'

Gilpin lifted his eyes to meet the mayor's gaze. 'Now just what does that mean?'

'Harry Digweed. He killed the man who shot Ben Casey, but it was him who strangled that Clark woman.'

'Who told you that?'

'It's all over town by now, I reckon, so we can consider the case closed. I understand you knew it was him but couldn't prove it. I guess there's a lot to be said for deathbed confessions. A man should clear his conscience with the Almighty before he dies.'

Gilpin doubted if the Almighty had anything to do with Harry's confession. The man had never been a believer.

Rickman looked up with a half smile on his face. 'So at least one of those killings is solved, eh, Sheriff?'

'Looks that way, don't it.'

The mayor drew in a deep breath, then eased it out again with deliberate control. 'Well, I must be off. Things to do. Just stopped by to congratulate you on your manhunt, Jeff.'

'The congratulations belong to Harry Digweed, Mr Mayor.'

'Quite so, quite so, but you know what I mean.' He paused in contemplation. 'Odd, when you come to think of it. Some folks had Rex Neeson down as that girl's killer. I hear somebody even hung a noose outside his bedroom window to let him know he wouldn't get away with it. Did you know about that?'

The sheriff was not about to admit that this was the first he had heard of it, so he said with a blank face, 'Reckon Neeson will be glad Harry confessed then.'

'I should imagine he will.'

The mayor went out and, as Gilpin stared at the closed door, he felt a sense of gratitude towards

Frank Walmsley. He had taken a load off his mind by resolving one of the most difficult problems Gilpin had ever faced.

Epilogue

Both Eli Atkins and Walt Martin were inclined to accept that Ezekiel Parker was indeed the offspring of the late Roger Talbot, taking into consideration the birth certificate Laura Parker had produced and the physical resemblance between the boy and his alleged father. Martin himself was willing to go along with the woman's claim that her son was now the rightful owner of the ranch he, Martin, had successfully managed for several years, having been assured that he would be retained in that capacity with an increase in salary. It was therefore not too difficult to persuade Ben Casey's widow, a timid woman, that she must surrender title of the store to the boy, especially when she was shown the legal document her husband had signed years earlier and she was assured that she would not be made homeless. Laura Parker agreed to let Mrs Casey run the store at an acceptable salary for as long as she was able to make it pay. Mrs Casey, with the help of her son Chris, was confident she could do this, both of them having learned from Ben how to buy goods at the best prices and sell them at a reasonable profit.

George Taggart and Chetwyn Handley were, however, a different proposition. They both dug in their heels and flatly refused to acknowledge that Ezekiel Parker had any right to ten per cent of their businesses. It was the boy himself who eventually persuaded his mother not to pursue them.

'It's enough, Ma, to have the ranch, the store, and the rents from the other properties, so don't fight them for what they don't want to give. We want to live in harmony with these people.'

And so it was that peace came again to Buzzards Creek.

John Henry 'Doc' Holliday left a few days after the killing of Horace Idle, thankful that he had been useful to his old friend on at least a couple of occasions. It was doubtful, he told Gilpin, if he would pass this way again.

'If this disease don't kill me before I'm forty, I reckon some fast gun will, Jeff.'

No one knew better than Sheriff Gilpin the truth of that and just a few years later conjecture became fact. 'Doc' Holliday survived the notorious Gunfight at the OK Corral in Arizona, but he died of tuberculosis in Glenwood Springs, Colorado, aged thirty-five, at ten o'clock one morning in November 1887.